I0694143

A Christmas Auction

A Christmas Auction

The Marriage Auction

By Audrey Carlan

A Christmas Auction
The Marriage Auction
By Audrey Carlan

Copyright 2024 Audrey Carlan
ISBN: 978-1-968707-61-3

Published by Blue Box Press, an imprint of Evil Eye Concepts, Incorporated

All rights reserved. No part of this book may be reproduced, scanned, or distributed in any printed or electronic form without permission. Please do not participate in or encourage piracy of copyrighted materials in violation of the author's rights.

This is a work of fiction. Names, places, characters and incidents are the product of the author's imagination and are fictitious. Any resemblance to actual persons, living or dead, events or establishments is solely coincidental.

Acknowledgments from the Author

This is my very first Christmas themed story! I genuinely loved dipping my toe into the waters of a holiday style novella. I hope you all loved it as much as I enjoyed writing it.

I always have to start by thanking Team AC. The women I have at my back and in my corner are my biggest strength. They keep me grounded, supported, and always make themselves available for my stories. I am eternally grateful for them and honored to have them as part of my writing process. I know I'm a better writer because of their feedback, critique, and continued love and friendship.

Tracey Wilson-Vuolo – Alpha Beta, Disney Freak, Proofer, ADA Expert

Tammy Hamilton-Green – Alpha Beta, Rock Chick, Plot Hole Finder, Educational Expert

Elaine Hennig – Alpha Beta, Brazilian Goddess, Medical Expert

Gabby McEachern - Alpha Beta, Dancing Queen, Spanish Expert

Dorothy Bircher – Alpha Beta, Mom Boss, Sensitivity Expert

Dannica Chiverrell – Admin Assistant, Niece, Gen Z Expert

Nicole Schwartz – Project Manager, Marketing Gal, Jack of all Trades

To **Ekaterina Sayanova**, my personal editor, you are the jelly to my peanut butter lady. I wouldn't be the writer I am today without your constant commitment to helping me hone my voice as a writer and storyteller. I love you, my friend.

To my literary agent, **Amy Tannenbaum** with Jane Rotrosen Agency, I am successful because you continue to believe in me and I in you. Together we're able to make magic. Let's just keep doing this for another decade or so. <wink>

To **Liz Berry**, **Jillian Stein**, and **MJ Rose** from Blue Box Press, with you three I found not only a sisterhood but a home. I never want to leave. Good luck kicking me out of my spot. I've already put up all my Taylor Swift posters and everything.

To **Stacey Tardif** and **Suzy Baldwin**, having copy editors from a publishing house work on your stories can be really stressful. It's such a private, personal, symbiotic relationship that's needed in order for us all to be on the same page. Somehow you both seamlessly add your sparkle to each book and create diamonds. I'm so grateful you continue to want to read and edit my stories. Thank you.

Dedication

This is dedicated to all the readers
that just want to read a sexy, smutty, sinful
little Christmas story to escape holiday hell.
You are my people.

Chapter 1

Deck the Halls

HOLLY

If I had to listen to this drunk sing Mariah Carey's "All I Want for Christmas" one more time, I'd be decking the halls by punching him in the face.

The out-of-towner swayed from side to side, alone in front of the old jukebox that was pay-to-play. He'd put the song on repeat, and it was playing for the fifth time in a row. As Christmas songs go, it was actually a good one. Most people liked it. But not at two in the morning with a dude in a wrinkled brown suit crooning along with the songbird—badly I might add—getting louder with each sip of the pint he was clutching to his chest.

Honestly, I felt bad for the guy. He'd been here all night, the day after Thanksgiving, getting absolutely shit-faced. While I had an amazing turkey day with my parents yesterday, gobbling up Mom's famous green bean casserole with fresh bits of prosciutto, a mouthwateringly juicy turkey Dad had fried to perfection, and my award-worthy garlic mashed potatoes, this guy looked like he'd had the worst couple days of his life.

The holidays could royally suck for those who didn't have someone special to spend them with. And unfortunately for him, before he'd taken to his solo dancing and singing career, he'd confided in me that his wife left him yesterday. On Thanksgiving Day, no less. Apparently, she was leaving him for a richer, younger man and taking their two kids with her. Which was what brought him here, to The Desert Shack on the outskirts of Las Vegas. He'd shared repeatedly how much he loved his wife and kids. The poor fella was devastated and drowning his sorrows with Mariah Carey and one beer after another. Overall, he was harmless, so I let him do his thing, even though I knew I'd have that song stuck in my head for the next week.

I scanned the bar, noting the few regulars finishing up their drinks and heading out without being urged. My regulars were awesome. Unlike the lumberjack at the end of the bar. He made my skin crawl. Mostly because he'd spent the entire evening staring at me nonstop and flirting with me relentlessly, even though I told him straight up that I wasn't interested. It wasn't that he was bad looking or anything. Technically, he was somewhat attractive in that dad-bod type of way, rocking a plaid shirt, jeans, and a full beard. Still, that didn't mean he was every woman's type. Good looks didn't automatically give him the right to persistently bother me while I was working, and besides, he gave me the ick. There was something off about him. My attempts to be nice throughout the night ended after the first couple hours of his skeevy behavior.

At this late hour though, I had ramped up to bold, brazen, and plum out of pleasantries. Putting my shoulders back, I took a deep breath, steeled my spine, and approached Mr. Bunyan.

"I'll have another," he barked, his salacious gaze traveling up and down my body. It felt like millions of ants racing across my bare skin.

"No can do." I gestured to the big round clock over the entrance to the bar that clearly showed it was ten minutes after two in the morning. "Last call was an hour ago," I reached for his empty whiskey glass. As I did so, he wrapped his hand around mine, squeezing painfully.

"I said, I'll have another…sweetness," he slurred. "Now hop that heart-shaped ass of yours over to the bottle of Jack and refill my glass."

"Let. Me. Go." I snarled, staring directly into his blood-shot, beady eyes.

He attempted a smirk, but it was more of a scowl hidden behind the swollen loose lips he kept licking.

"You heard the woman," drunken Christmas singer hollered, waving his pint, the amber liquor sloshing onto the floor. "She said to get your hand off her. So you know"—he stumbled awkwardly—"let her go, man."

Mr. Bunyan's eyes narrowed, and he turned slowly around, finally removing his hand from mine. I snatched it away and went over toward the cash register where I hid my rifle. I could already tell this was going to be one of those nights.

Before I could intervene, the lumberjack stood up, a solid six inches taller than my drunken savior, pulled his arm back and clocked the guy in the face with his meaty fist.

I swear I saw it happen in slow motion.

Christmas guy's head flew to the side with the force of the blow, blood spewing from his mouth while his body fell to the floor. He scrambled to a seated position, his hand covering the split in his lip as blood trailed down his chin. The beer mug he'd been holding had also fallen to the floor and shattered, the bits of glass spreading along the rickety wooden surface like sparkly diamonds.

That's when I cocked my rifle and pointed it at Mr. Bunyan.

"Time to go or you'll be lying on the floor bleeding from a far bigger wound than my friend there." I jerked the gun toward the door. "Leave now, and I won't call the cops on you for assaulting a customer."

"You're gonna regret this, sweetness," he growled, his chest moving up and down as though he'd run a marathon. "We could'a had a good time together," he continued, licking his gross lips once more.

"I sincerely doubt that. Now go and don't ever come back. If I see you again, it will be to place this rifle right between your eyes."

The nostrils on his bulbous nose flared, reminding me of Rudolph the Red Nosed Reindeer, his eyes blacker than night as he snarled. "I'll be seeing you…"

"Over my dead body," I snapped as he walked calmly and slowly to the exit.

"That can be arranged." He grinned, a malicious smile that sent shivers racing down my back. My knees shook but I stayed strong, my rifle still pointed at him.

"Says the one without the gun," I hollered as he disappeared behind the door and out into the parking lot.

"Fuck me!" Christmas guy rolled over onto all fours as he tried to make it to his feet. "I'm such a loser. I can't hold onto my wife and kids, and I can't even help a nice bartender."

I came around the bar and set the rifle on top of the counter so that I could help him up onto a barstool. I grabbed a stack of cocktail napkins and shoved them into his hand. "Here, staunch the flow. I'll call you a cab."

"Thanks, lady."

"Holly," I corrected, pushing my long blonde hair out of my face.

"Holly. That's a nice name. Very Christmasy," he mumbled

around the napkins he'd pressed against his wound. "I love Christmas," he moaned.

I snickered, wanting to tell him I had been referring to him as Christmas guy all night in my head but thought better of it. He might not see it as a compliment, and he'd already had a shit night. I got him a tall glass of water then proceeded to call him a cab. He was in no position to be driving and didn't so much as suggest otherwise. He simply brooded while I cleaned up the broken glass, picked up the empties, then put all the chairs on the tables for the cleaning crew that would come in the morning.

At least I didn't have to clean the bar before I could crash. That was one rule I'd made when the owner offered me the position of manager. It came with a one-bedroom studio above the bar, and a cleaning service to wash the dishes, bathrooms, floors, and all of the tables before the first-shift bartender started at three p.m. Mac was the only other employee that worked at The Desert Shack. He came in early, made sure the kegs were full or changed out, all the brew was stocked, and inventory checked before we opened at five p.m. My shift technically started at six every evening, but I usually helped where I could. Mostly because I liked Mac. He was an ex-con and a biker that ran with the Las Vegas Hounds. He'd offered many times to take on the night shift, but that's when the tips are the best, so I'd declined. Plus, I knew he liked to hang out with his club brothers in the evenings.

Mac treated me like I was his little sister, as did the many bikers from his club that came to drink, play darts, and jam out to 80s rock such as AC/DC, Van Halen, Aerosmith, and Ozzy Osborn. I loved those days, because 80s music was awesome. But, since it was the Friday after Thanksgiving, the club was spending time with their old ladies and the biker bunnies. Boy Mac would be pissed if he heard about the lumberjack sitch.

After I counted out the evening's cash, while still waiting

for the cab for my drunken customer, I thought about what I really wanted for Christmas this year. The answer was always the same…to open my own bar.

For the past five years, I'd saved every penny and tip possible toward achieving that goal. I'd taken business courses online, and flawlessly ran this rinky-dink place to the best of my ability, but I wanted more. At thirty years old, I *needed* more.

I wanted a real life. One I was proud of. A career of my own making. I had thirty grand saved but it wasn't enough. The banks said I needed a few hundred thousand to open a new, hip bar in the city of Las Vegas.

What I really needed was an investor—or a miracle.

A honking horn broke me from my reverie. I grabbed my handy-dandy taser as I put back my rifle and clipped the taser to the front of my jeans. A girl could never be too careful exiting into a parking lot at night, and my drunken customer would need assistance.

"That's your cue, my friend," I said as I walked around the bar and held out my arm. He clutched me around my shoulders, a bit wobbly on his feet.

"I'm sorry I broke your glass, and I wasn't much help with that guy," he shared miserably.

I smiled at him as I helped him out the front door. "No, you were a perfect gentleman. But word of advice…" I said as he opened the bright yellow cab's door.

"Yeah?" He turned bleary, sorrow-filled eyes in my direction.

"Lay off the Mariah Carey." I grinned.

He burst into laughter but then immediately winced, pressing his handful of bloody napkins back to his lip. "Ouch. And noted. I'll pick up my car tomorrow. Thanks for, you know, being kind."

I patted his shoulder. "You too. Good luck."

"Thanks, I'll need it." He groaned and his head flopped

back against the seat as I shut the door and slapped the top of car.

The driver didn't even spare me a glance before they jetted off.

A cool breeze cascaded along my bare arms as I took in the parking lot and breathed in the cool desert air. There were multiple cars left in the lot, which wasn't unusual at a bar. Lots of people imbibed more than they should and caught a ride home then picked up their cars the next day. Usually, by the time I left the building to run my errands in the late morning, all the cars would be gone.

For a moment, I closed my eyes and lifted my head to the sky, allowing the stress of the night to leave my body one quiet second at a time.

I wasn't prepared for the arms that suddenly wrapped around me from behind. One hand covered my mouth while the other arm locked around my upper body, slamming my back into a male chest. Instantly, I started to fight against the giant who held me trapped.

"What did I say, you little tease?" The booming voice of the lumberjack sneered against my cheek, the stench of stale beer and something sour flooded my senses, while fear, caked in the need for survival, rose to the surface from within me.

I screamed behind the hand he held over my mouth, but no one remotely close would hear it. I was utterly alone and about to experience my worst nightmare coming true.

We were out in the middle of nowhere. But like a light at the end of a long, dark tunnel, I saw a pair of headlights headed this way from the direction of the old airport. Lots of rich men and women with private planes used that airstrip now that it had been revamped and was under new ownership after it had been the location of a violent mafia war.

Maybe the person in the car could help…

I kicked and scratched at the lumberjack with every ounce

of energy I could muster.

He only held me tighter, one of his beefy sweaty fingers pushing between my lips. The taste of salt and grease made me gag but also gave me an idea. I took the chance and opened my mouth wider. As I'd hoped, his finger slid inside, and I bit down as hard as I could, tasting the metallic flavor of blood and feeling the crunch of bone.

My attacker howled in pain and let me go. In a flash, I spun around screaming at the top of my lungs while waving my hands in the air with the hopes of getting the attention of the car driving by. I started to run in the direction of the road, willing to put my body in front of that car rather than be left alone with my attacker. Before I could make it a solid fifteen feet, another man came barreling out of nowhere, and slammed the full weight of his large body into mine. I flew to the side, my hip and palms crashing to the ground as I skidded across the gravel, bits of rock and dirt digging painfully into my palms.

I ripped the taser from my pants and just barely got my trembling fingers on the trigger before I was yanked up by the roots of my hair.

I screeched, reaching for the hand that was gripping my hair. Pain like I'd never felt before made me feel like every piece of hair was being brutally ripped out at the same time. I shoved an arm back behind me and touched the taser blindly to my attacker then pressed the trigger.

His hand instantly loosened, and his body jolted like a live wire before falling to the ground.

That's when all hell broke loose.

A shiny black limo rumbled through the parking lot at high speed right as I was tackled a second time by the lumberjack. We rolled on the ground until he was on top, straddling me, his knees on my upper arms pinning me.

"You fucking bitch! How dare you taze my brother! I'll kill you!" he bellowed, his monster-sized hands squeezing my throat.

I kicked my legs, rocks flying all around as I heard yelling. Then a gunshot blast pierced the air. The lack of oxygen took over, my vision going in and out while stars flickered and blurred at the edges of my vision.

I was seconds away from losing consciousness when the vise around my neck disappeared and magical, crisp, cool air entered my lungs. I gasped greedily as hazy figures moved around me.

"*Chérie?*" A light tapping on my cheek made me blink several times. I was trying to stay awake…trying to stay alive. "I fear she needs medical attention," a lilting French accent said as the blurry image of a petite woman hovered over my face. Her fingers were cool to the touch as she traced my eyebrows and cupped my cheek gently. "It is okay. You are safe. We're going to help you," she said, and I believed her. I recognized that voice. I'd heard it before, so I held onto that bit of safety like a lifeline.

I moaned as the various bumps, bruises, and gashes made themselves known, sending pain soaring through every inch of my body.

It hurt.

Everywhere.

"I've got her." A growly, bear-like voice. Then I was lifted up into a pair of strong arms. I tried to stay awake, I really did, but as I was brought into a car and placed in the cradle of a warm embrace, my eyes became unbearably heavy. Still, as I opened and closed my eyes, all I could see was the face of a man.

Dark wavy hair that flipped and flopped around a stern expression. Eyes that were the deepest espresso brown. A beard and mustache combo that looked so soft I wanted to touch it.

I lifted my hand and pressed my fingers to his soft, full, pink lips.

"You're beautiful," I whispered and then promptly passed out.

Chapter 2

A Christmas Miracle

BRUNO

I paced the halls of the hospital, waiting to hear something about the blonde stranger we happened upon on our way to the hotel from the private airstrip. I didn't even know how Alana Toussaint, otherwise known as *Madam Alana,* had conned me into this gig. Security management for the very private, very sought after Christmas Auction she held once a year was not my typical contract. If it wasn't for my cousin, Joel, demanding I accept the job on behalf of the Castellanos' good name, I'd be somewhere in the Maldives, hunting down an art thief that had stolen a priceless artifact from another one of my clients.

How a person could put themselves up for a marriage auction to the highest bidder for a period of three years was outrageous to me. Even more shocking was the price tag these candidates went for. No less than three mil a bid, with most of these individuals going for far higher. Hell, even my cousin Joel found his beloved wife, Faith, through this process. And what a shitshow that was. Kidnappings, mafia, a gunfight, exploding planes, not to mention the dozens of lives lost in that battle was not a situation I wanted to relive.

Whatever happened to meeting someone the old-fashioned way? See a cute girl from across the room, buy said girl a drink, and *voila*, you've got the start of something. Then again, if that worked, I'd be married a dozen times already. Yet, I wasn't the target audience for marriage. I never planned on getting married. It wasn't that I was opposed to a forever type of love, it's just that particular concept didn't fit in with my lifestyle. Commitment was *not* my thing. Which is why I hadn't been in a "relationship" with a woman other than the occasional bar hookup, in a solid decade. And at thirty-four, my options of changing that weren't looking any brighter.

I loved my work more than the idea of love. Perhaps it's because I haven't ever been in love. The type of woman I could truly fall for would have to be one in a billion. She'd have to be self-sufficient and prefer to spend more time on her own than with her partner. The work I did often took me all over the world for extended periods of time. It wasn't conducive to what society considered a marriage between lovers.

My company was a hundred-million-dollar elite security service that wasn't for the faint of heart or people with slim pocketbooks. Contracting with my outfit was designed for individuals that carried around shiny black Amex cards with no limits. Not to mention the high-risk environment I often found myself in. For example, the last job I was on had me working with the Latin Mafia to take down a Russian mobster who'd killed several innocents connected to friends of mine.

What woman could handle the type of man who had a job that often required the skills needed by an ex-military special operative?

Not a single woman I'd ever met.

"She's waking up," Alana called out, waving me over.

I wasn't even sure why I was still here. Alana, her driver, and I had already given our statements to the authorities regarding the two guys that had attacked the sleeping beauty. There really wasn't anything more for me to do, yet I moved one foot in front of the other to the entrance of the hospital room as though tethered to the woman. I *needed* to ensure her safety. Seeing her bruised and battered by a couple of assholes broke something inside of me wide open I didn't know how to explain. And I certainly wasn't prepared to dig any deeper into my psyche at that moment. I'd leave that bit of self-reflection for when I was alone with a glass of whiskey firmly clutched in my hand.

Alana was already by the woman's bedside, her hand on the stunning blonde's forearm, keeping clear of her bandaged palms. Sure, I'd noticed how damn gorgeous the stranger was. She'd passed out in my arms for chrissake. What was I to look at beside her unique features? High cheekbones, full pink lips, long slim nose, perfectly arched wheat-colored eyebrows that matched the long golden locks of her hair. But none of that prepared me for the combination of all of that paired together with the most serene, warm, brown eyes. They reminded me of the desert first thing in the morning, the earthy color striking against her skin tone.

"Holly, dearest, are you well? Shall I get the doctor?" Alana asked in that eloquent French lilt of hers that made people with the harshest of personalities and a chip on their shoulder relax at the comforting sound.

Holly.

A lovely name for knockout of a woman.

She blinked a few times, her brows furrowing as she assessed Alana. "It was you who stopped?"

Alana smiled and patted Holly's arm while nodding.

"You saved me?" she croaked, her bottom lip trembling.

I gritted my teeth, hating seeing the emotional turmoil that flooded Holly's face. Her eyes pooled with unshed tears.

Alana shook her head. "No, *chérie*, Bruno saved you." She smiled and then shifted her body so Holly could see me better.

"Bruno?" Her tone sounded confused as she sought me out. The moment our gazes met, my heart started to pound an unfamiliar staccato beat.

I lifted my chin in recognition but didn't dare approach. She'd been roughly attacked by two men. Seeing another unknown male could make her feel unsafe. Just witnessing her uncertain and fragile, lying in a hospital bed after being terrified and assaulted made me want to pound my fist into that drunkard's face all over again. This time until he had no recognizable face left.

Holly shifted her body, wincing as Alana helped her raise the back of the bed, maneuvering her in a seated position.

"Thank you," Holly said, her voice a bit raw. "For everything. I can only imagine what could have…" she shivered, and I could see her mind spinning with what might have been, had we not intervened.

"No," I clipped, raising my hand in a stop speaking gesture. "No thanks needed. I'm glad you're okay Miz…"

"Holly Knight. And you are?"

"Bruno Castellanos." I filled a cup of water at the sink and handed it to Alana, still keeping my distance.

Alana offered Holly the cup, and she drank swiftly.

"Why were you on my side of town so late at night anyway?" Holly asked.

That's when Alana's lips shifted into that impish grin. I could already see the gears turning.

"Funny you should ask, *chérie*. I had planned on making a visit to your establishment tomorrow in fact."

"To see me? Why?"

"To discuss a matter of great import. You remember when we first met, and you told me about your dreams to own your own bar in the heart of Las Vegas proper?"

Holly frowned, brought her hand up toward her forehead then stopped mid-air, seemingly noticing for the first time her hands were bandaged. She carefully lowered them to her lap.

"Um, kinda. Then you came in with your husband and we…"

"Discussed how all you needed was a large loan from the bank, but they wouldn't approve you because you were unmarried with limited resources," Alana finished.

Holly's cheeks flared the prettiest shade of pink as her gaze flicked to mine, clearly embarrassed at Alana's candor. Though she needn't have been. Starting up a new business venture wasn't easy. Especially when trying to go the bank loan route. Most banks wouldn't take a risk, especially with a single individual without a proven track record for success.

"I couldn't accept a loan from you. We barely know one another," Holly countered.

"Agreed. However, I am willing to offer you a very coveted position within my own business that will provide you with all the capital you need to make your dreams come true. Call it a Christmas miracle if you wish."

"I'm confused. You and your friend here, saved me from two men who wanted to hurt me in a way I likely would never recovery from, provided they didn't kill me, and now you want to offer me an opportunity to make enough money to see my dreams come to fruition?" She looked at the medical equipment and the IV hanging above her bed. "They must be giving me the good drugs. I think I'm hallucinating."

Alana chuckled, and it sounded like whimsical chimes blowing in the wind. "I assure you, you are not hallucinating." She pulled out a matte black business card and set it on the end table nearest the bed. "I'm going to leave this here. When you are feeling better tomorrow, give me a call and we can discuss this further."

"But I…"

"Oh my God! Holly!" a woman that looked almost identical to Holly screeched as she raced into the room. A stout man with grayish-blond hair followed not far behind, his face drawn in what could only be sorrow and fear.

The parents.

The woman's hair was cut into a shoulder length bob. She was dressed in a tight black skirt that hit her mid-thigh. She wore black pantyhose and black sneakers. On top was a tuxedo shirt with a black bowtie. The father was dressed similarly, though he had on suspenders with his crisp white dress shirt and black satin tie. They looked like they just needed a red jacket with gold buttons, and they'd be ready for their circus act. Technically, we were in Vegas, so it wasn't outside the realm of possibility, but they were far too old for that type of work.

"Mom! Dad!" Holly held both of her arms out and her parents went on either side of the bed to embrace their daughter.

"My baby! Oh, thank the good Lord you're okay. What happened?" her mother asked.

Alana backed up and came to my side, then proceeded to take my elbow as though I was her escort. "We'll just be on our way," she announced.

"Oh, no! I want you to meet my saviors," Holly stated. "Mom, Dad, this is Alana Toussaint and Bruno Castellanos. These two stopped in the middle of the night when I was being attacked by two men. They saved me. Bruno even took one of them out," Holly gushed. "The other, I tased, just like you taught me."

"You were attacked by *two* men?" Her mother sobbed, tears tracking down her face. "I told you that place was danger-ous, honey. All the way out there on the outskirts of town, and you live and work there."

Holly's father left her side and approached us. He stood tall and put out his hand. "Adam Knight. I can't thank you enough for protecting our girl."

We both shook his hand while her mother approached.

"Noelle Knight," she said, and instead of taking my hand she waved it away and flung her arms around my shoulders then pulled me into a tight hug.

"May God bless you with all you desire. Thank you. Thank you for saving our only child." She pulled back, cupped both of my cheeks and smiled. She was a beautiful woman, and her gratitude made her effervescent, mirroring where Holly got her good looks from.

"It was the right thing to do," I murmured, feeling uncomfortable with all the praise. "Shall we?" I gestured to the exit, my need to flee this emotional scene becoming more compelling the longer Holly's grateful expression and pretty eyes searched mine.

"Holly, don't forget to call." Alana said as the happy family embraced once more.

The second we'd made our way through the hospital and out into the cool desert air, I let out the breath I'd been holding.

Alana laughed as we waited for her driver to roll up. "Uncomfortable in hospitals?" she asked nonchalantly.

"You could say that" I grunted.

"Or perhaps it was the beautiful woman you saved. Did Holly wiggle her way under your skin? She's very pretty…"

"Alana…don't," I warned. "I'm not here as a bidder nor a candidate in one of your auctions. I'm perfectly capable of finding a woman all on my own if that was, in fact, something I desired."

"Do you not desire a woman such as Holly Knight? I'd assume a woman like that was your type."

"That woman is everyone's type."

"Then what's the problem?" She turned to face me and crossed her arms over one another, one of her black brows arched in question.

"We're not having this conversation," I stated with an ounce of annoyance, so she'd get the hint.

"And why not?" Her voice rose slightly.

"Because I am only here to provide you with the security and invasive background checks you demand for each of your candidates and bidders. Remember the catastrophe that occurred in France months ago? You were the one that called in this favor. Do not think for a moment you're going to drag me into a matchmaking scenario. I am not in the market for a bride. Not now, not ever. Got it?"

Alana tilted her head and stared at me for a solid ten seconds, likely choosing her words wisely. "Such an impassioned speech for someone who is…*not in the market*." She enunciated the last part as though it was a challenge.

"Well, I'm passionate about not getting married."

"Hmmm," she hummed as the car drove up.

I opened the passenger door for her, the two of us standing on opposite sides of the door. Two strong personalities staring one another down.

"I guess we shall see how the month goes." She pursed her lips.

"Guess we shall."

Chapter 3

The Christmas Auction

HOLLY

"I'm fine, Mom. Really. It's been three days of nothing but being fawned over by you and Dad. You don't have enough vacation time saved up from the casino to stay home any longer. And it's time I get back to The Desert Shack and my own life."

"Now Holly, you can't rush these things. Healing takes time. And your dad and I have worked at the casino for over twenty years. When the other waitresses heard what happened to you, they all chipped in to cover my shifts. I've got it handled. Don't worry about me," she chattered on.

Mom was in her element. Taking care of me was her greatest joy. I know that because she repeated it regularly. If they could have afforded it, the entire house would have been filled with children, but they decided early on in their marriage that one was enough for them. Sometimes I wished they'd had other children, then I wouldn't be the center of their universe.

I gritted my teeth as Mom brought me another pillow I didn't need. For the past three days I'd been laid out on my parents' couch, with them hovering over me like I was five years old again.

"How does chicken soup, Saltines, and 7-Up sound for lunch?" She hummed merrily as she headed to the kitchen to make soup.

"Mom, I'm not sick. I was attacked by a couple of drunken criminals who are sitting in jail right now." I stood up, shucked off the blanket, and marched into the kitchen. "I'm going to take a shower and head back to my place. You and Dad have been amazing as usual, but I need to go home."

"Baby, this is your home." She opened her arms wide, gesturing to the tiny kitchen in the two-bedroom duplex they'd rented my entire life. Thankfully, they had a good landlord and were lucky that he used this property as a tax write-off without raising the rent too much over the years.

My parents lived a happy, simple, rather uncomplicated life here in Vegas. Dad was a card dealer and Mom was a cocktail waitress. They met in a casino, and they've spent their entire relationship working in one. I knew how to play poker before I knew my ABCs. I also knew and respected the golden rule in Las Vegas. *The house always wins.* Sure, you could get "lucky", if you want to call it that, and maybe pull a lever and win a jackpot or roll the right numbers in craps, but that wasn't the norm. Casinos were in business for one reason. To make money. And they did that very well. I just wished they provided better for their staff. Mom and Dad were happy, but for the most part, they lived paycheck to paycheck with just enough extra to go out of town once a year on vacation and no retirement.

One day, if I was ever able to start up my own flashy bar, I'd send them on a real vacation. For years, Mom dreamed of going to Paris, but on their income, that was a pipe dream. Sometimes I thought about burning my savings and taking all three of us on a trip of a lifetime, and if I didn't start making my dreams a reality soon, I might just cave and do it.

"I know this will always be my home because it's where you and Dad are. But Mom, home isn't a place, it's the people you love. And we all deserve more in life. You and Dad deserve more and one day, somehow, I'm going to make it happen."

She came over to me, cupped my cheeks and smiled. "I have faith in you, Holly. If opening your own establishment will fill this void in your soul, your father and I are happy to support you in it. Whatever that entails."

I put my hands over hers. "Then you have to let me go back to work. Neither one of us is making tips hanging out on the couch and watching old movies."

"It's just…" her breath hitched. "When we got that call you were in the hospital… Holly, I'd never been more scared in my entire life. Not ever."

Tears filled both of our eyes as that reminder struck a chord between us. "I know, but it all worked out. I know better how to protect myself and will make sure I stay completely alert and aware from now on."

"Okay," she sighed. "I'll pack your things while you shower. But, baby, you know you're always welcome back home. Anytime you need us, we're right here."

I pulled her into a big hug, snuggling against her neck, her perfume filling my senses with the familiar white amber, lavender, and apple scent that was *Lovely* by Sarah Jessica Parker. It was supposed to remind the wearer of that old hit show *Sex and the City*. Mom was obsessed with SJP the way people were with Taylor Swift. I thought it was cute, and I enabled her fascination by buying her a bottle of perfume every year on Mother's Day.

And every year, she acted as if it was the first time I bought it for her.

My mom was the best. And as I let her go and made my way to the shower, I vowed to one day give her that trip of a lifetime. Maybe we could also go to New York City first and hit all the places SJP did in the show. My mother would lose her mind.

As I pulled back the shower curtain, removed my clothes, and turned on the water, I stepped inside with one thing on my mind.

How could I make a lot of money in a short amount of time?

Pinching my pennies and saving all my tips to put $6,000 in the bank every year wasn't nearly enough. It would never be enough.

I needed a miracle.

When I got back to the bar, Mac was already there. He wore a black bandana tied around his bald head, a white T-shirt, his leather cut, and a pair of ratty jeans and black combat boots. Basically, his normal uniform. He had a salt and pepper mustache that I'd been told was called a Fu Manchu style because it was bushy around his upper lip and went down the sides of his mouth, stopping at his jawline. I thought it was badass and so did the myriad forty and fifty-something biker babes that often waited for him to end his shift each night he worked.

"Hey Mac," I waved as I dragged in my duffle bag.

He pressed his big hands to the bar top, bracing his giant frame. The guy was six foot four, at least two hundred and sixty pounds, and had a mean resting dick face.

"Don't you *Hey Mac* me, little girl!" he bit out angrily.

I stopped in my tracks. "Well hello to you too. Who pissed in your cheerios this morning?"

"Don't you dare give me that bullshit," he growled, his tone rising as his face reddened.

"Mac, what's wrong?"

His body jerked as though he'd been struck. "Are you fucking kidding me right now?"

"Mac, I'm sensing some hostility—"

"You were fucking attacked!" he raged. "At our bar! And you didn't CALL ME!" he roared, clearly pissed right the fuck off.

My shoulders slumped as I realized what was happening. "Mac, seriously, I'm fine. You're overreacting."

"Overreacting," he sneered. "You haven't seen overreacting, but you will," he threatened. "No one messes with Hound property and lives to talk about it."

"I'm not Hound property."

"The fuck you aren't," he countered, spitball flying alongside his fury.

"Mac, really. It wasn't that bad..." I began, attempting to de-escalate the situation.

He spoke through his teeth. "My sources tell me it was the Baskin brothers. Two men that are twice your size, came onto Hound turf and roughed up one of ours? And you tell me I'm overreacting? Are you fucking kidding me!"

I walked over to the bar and set my duffle on one of the stools. "Mac, listen to me," I tried again.

"No! You listen, Holly. You may not realize the severity of the situation, because you're sweet. And me and my brothers protect sweet. But"—he pointed at my chest—"no one messes with you." Then he pointed at the bar top. "Or this bar as long as it's in Hound's territory."

"Don't worry, they've been taken to jail. My guess, they'll be in there for a while."

He reached out and took my hand and gave it a squeeze. I couldn't help the instant wince and hiss of pain that left my lips, because my palms were still healing.

His eyes flared with white-hot fire as he turned over my hand and saw the abrasions from when I skidded across the gravel multiple times.

Gently, he grabbed my other hand and turned it palm up. He dipped his head and placed a featherlight kiss on each one just like a father or a big brother would for his daughter or little sister.

"I'm going to fucking kill them with my bare hands," he rumbled so low I could feel that vow thunder through my chest like an incoming storm.

Shit. The last thing I needed were the Hounds involved. Even if they meant well, I suspected they got into a lot of illegal activity, and I wanted no part of that lifestyle.

"Mac, please, I'm okay. Really." I pulled my hands out of his grasp. "I just want to forget all of this ever happened and get back to work."

He nodded, his jaw firm, his eyes wild. I didn't know if he'd listen to me, but at that moment, I just wanted to move forward.

Unsurprisingly, that night, the entire The Las Vegas Hounds motorcycle club was in attendance. Each one of them spoke kindly to me, overtipped, and eyed every last man that entered the bar. Until one of the sexiest women alive entered. Then all eyes were on her.

"God damn," Mac breathed as Alana Toussaint entered, wearing a fierce all-white business suit that hugged every inch of her lithe form. A pair of red four-inch stilettos made the outfit not only fashion-forward but edgy. Her black hair was parted down the center and fell in a flat glossy sheet down her back. Her eyes were lined with kohl in a vicious cat-eye shape I'd always wanted to learn but never got the hang of. Her hips swayed from side to side, mesmerizing every biker in the room. She smiled coyly as she approached the bar, her cherry-red lips looking positively edible. She was a force of nature, and I desperately wanted to know her secret.

"*Bonjour, chérie*," she said as she waved at the stool in front of me.

Sam, a hot biker that had been hitting on me for years, promptly got up and out of his seat to help Alana get settled.

"*Merci.*" Alana smiled sweetly and then sat, placing a slim, red leather wristlet wallet onto the counter. "I believe you know what I like."

Mac leaned forward. "I'd be happy to make it my business to give you anything you'd like, beautiful," he said using that biker charm that wooed the biker chicks.

I shoved Mac aside. "Don't even start," I warned. "I happen to know for a fact she's married to a hot French guy. Christopher? No, Christophe." I tried to remember the man she introduced me to the second time I saw her. Now that I was out of the hospital and in my right mind, I remembered exactly when we'd first met. Her limo had blown a tire. She drank tequila and chatted about life while her driver took care of the problem. Then she'd come in a second time a month or so later, with her husband, to have a nightcap.

Mac covered his heart with both his hands. "Say it ain't so, beautiful?"

"I'm afraid it is. Married thirty years and counting."

"Happily?" he hedged, and she nodded.

"Dude, seriously?" I laughed.

"Hey, a man has to shoot his shot when the most beautiful woman alive walks into the bar." He confirmed my exact thoughts. She was something else.

"I thought *I* was the most beautiful woman alive." I crossed my arms and playfully glared at him.

"You're the most beautiful *blonde* I've ever known. But I don't want to fuck you. You're like my sister. You're hot, but again…" He grimaced. "Too sisterly, blech." He shivered as though grossed out.

"You suck!" I bumped his hip with my own and then remembered that was the bruised one. "Ouch! Damn it all to hell in a handbasket." I moaned in pain, rubbing my hip.

Mac's hands instantly curled into fists. "So, your hip is fucked up too? Not just your hands or those elbows that are nasty looking and barely scabbing over. Not to mention, you keep touching the crown of your head as if just the weight of your hair hurts. That only happens when someone is pulled around by their hair forcefully. Is that what they did to you? Hmmm? I want every detail, Holly."

I turned around and placed my hands to Mac's broad shoulders and looked him dead in the eye. "I'm okay. I'm right here. Alive and well. Just a few bumps and scrapes. No worries. We're having fun. The entire freakin' club is here. Enjoy your brethren while I talk to Alana."

"Alana? Pretty name for a pretty lady." He waggled his eyebrows in her direction.

"*Merci,*" her lips pressed together, and she looked down and away while tapping red painted nails on the bar top rather seductively. Although, I didn't think being sexy or enthralling was her intent. The woman just oozed confidence, elegance, and unbelievable beauty.

"Mac, please," I begged, staring into his eyes.

"Fine," he grated through his teeth. "I'll drop it, for now. Tomorrow, all bets are off."

I groaned and then went over to the most expensive bottle of tequila we served and poured two shots a piece into two different glasses. Then I grabbed a couple wedges of lime and plonked them on the rims of each glass. I set one in front of Alana and then picked up the other for myself.

She smiled, showing all her white perfect teeth. "To new opportunities."

"Sure," I shrugged and clinked her glass then shot the entire double while she sipped hers primly. The alcoholic burn sliding down my throat was the liquid courage I needed to get through the evening with Mac and his brothers brooding about what happened to me. "Soooo, thanks again for what you and your friend Bruno did the other night. The drink is on me tonight. Actually, every time you come in your drinks are on me. If you hadn't shown up, things could have been very different. I'm really grateful you had my back. It looks like you are my fairy godmother after all."

Alana chuckled whimsically and set down her drink. "Technically, a fairy godmother would have more to offer than assistance fending off a couple bad men. And besides, that was all you and Bruno. I just happened to be in the car at the right time."

"Well, I'm still grateful. But that doesn't give me any hints as to what brings you here tonight."

"I have something I'd like to discuss with you. Is there somewhere private we could chat?"

"Sure. My place is just upstairs." I pointed above our head.

"You live here? Over the bar?" That time it was Alana who

put her hand over her heart.

What was it about me that made everyone react as though I was shocking them left and right?

"Yep. Come on. You can bring your drink. I'm going to pour myself another." For some reason, I felt I was going to need even more courage than I previously anticipated. "Mac, I'm going upstairs for a bit. Cover for me."

He waved me off like batting away a gnat. Rude.

Alana followed me around the bar, through the back door, and up a set of stairs. I pulled out my key and unlocked my door. I always kept it locked up tight while I worked, just in case someone tried to slip up the stairs without my notice.

I gestured to the small round table with four chairs tucked underneath it. My studio apartment was laid out really well and the square footage matched the entire size of the bar. When you walked in, my bedroom space was on the left. I had a queen-sized bed placed against the wall along with a nightstand and a pair of matching lamps on either side. Purposely, I had my dad rig up floor-to-ceiling bookcases to create a divide between my room and the living space. We removed the back panel of the bookcases so that you could see through them, making the space seem even bigger.

In the center of the room, I had a single couch that faced a faux fireplace and mantle. Within the insert I'd placed an electric fireplace that actually put out some heat, and I adored the flickering light. Above that was my TV. Pictures of my family and friends dotted the mantle along with some candlesticks. To the right of the entrance and the living room was my small kitchen. It was an L-shape leaving the rest of the space open, so that's where I put the tiny four-seater table. I never wanted to live in a place where I couldn't have my parents sit down and share a meal with me.

Alana took a seat at the table, sat up straight and crossed her legs.

I plopped into the seat opposite her. "So, what do you want to talk about?"

"I want to talk about you, *chérie*. When we first met, you said you wanted to own your own bar."

"That's right…"

"And that you'd been saving, but the banks wouldn't loan you the money you requested."

"Yep. That's my life in a nutshell."

"What if I offered you the opportunity to earn no less than three million dollars, over the course of a three-year period."

"I'd say you're either lying, clinically psychotic, or a criminal."

Alana grinned wide. "I assure you I am none of those things."

"Then what business are you in?"

"I run an elite auction, completely legal, and guaranteed to secure you the money you need."

"What do you auction? Art?" I asked.

"In a way, I do auction off one-of-a-kind beauties."

"If not art, then what?"

"Marriage, *chérie*."

"Marriage. As in you set up arranged marriages?" I frowned, sat back in my chair and ran my hand through my hair. The roots still throbbed painfully.

"More like, a marriage auction. In this particular case, an auction that will be hosted on Christmas Eve. A Christmas Auction."

"Okay, I'm afraid I'm not really following. Who's getting married?"

That's when she smiled so big it was as though she glowed from the inside out.

"You, my dear."

Chapter 4

Ho, Ho, Ho, Merry Freakin' Christmas

HOLLY

Without even saying a single word, I reached across the table, grabbed the rest of Alana's tequila and shot the damn thing straight back, looking for that burn to shock my heart back into beating.

Alana, as suspected, didn't so much as flinch. The woman was as cool as a cucumber while my internal temperature skyrocketed and sweat beaded at my hairline and underneath my arms.

"You want to—" I gulped, not being able to suck in enough air as the dots of what she just explained connected in my mind.

I jumped up, fanning my suddenly flushed face, and went to the window over the sink. I was too fucking hot. My fingers scrambled to unlock the rusted hinge and shove the damn thing open. But once I did, a blessedly cool desert breeze smacked me in the face. I inhaled deeply several times, letting the chilly air cool my heated skin. Putting my hands to the edge of the sink, I braced myself and turned my head to look at Alana.

As I'd come to expect, she was sitting quietly and rather elegantly in my kitchen chair, her body and face the epitome of relaxed feminine beauty. I, on the other hand, was losing my shit.

"You want to put *me*, Holly Knight, up for auction? For marriage?"

"*Oui, chérie.* That is correct." She blinked prettily.

"A marriage auction. So I would what, stand up, like on a stage, and have men bid on me? Like cattle?"

Alana shook her head. "No, Holly. Not like cattle. More like art. Living, breathing, art."

I shook my head, reached for a glass that had been drying in the rack next to the sink, filled it with water and glugged it down.

"I don't get it."

Alana patted the table. "Why don't you sit down? We'll discuss the finer details, and maybe I can relieve any concerns you might have."

"Might have. I can think of a hundred concerns. The first one being how is this legal?"

"Darling, arranged marriages happen every day all over the world. This is not a new concept, I assure you."

"Not to me, they don't," I scoffed.

Alana merely pressed her lips together and waited patiently for me to quiet down. Reminded me of when I was back in grade school and I'd just been scolded by the teacher for speaking out of turn. Alana didn't even have to say anything when her facial expression and patient silence said it all for her.

I clamped my big mouth shut.

"Let me go over the primary details. The rest is laid out in a contract that both the candidate and bidder have to sign prior to the auction. I promise you, everything is entirely legal—and most importantly—*safe*. I have been in this business for thirty years. I met my husband in a marriage auction."

I gasped. "You and Christophe?"

"It seems like a lifetime ago," she said with a level of whimsy to her features I hadn't yet seen. "Truly, it was the best decision I ever made. We were fortunate enough to fall in love rather quickly, and beyond that, I had the financial security I needed. It is what led me to purchase the marriage auction from the original owner. He wasn't running a legal or safe business. Now, when I have a male or female candidate enter the auction, they are my priority. Their happiness and safety is crucial to my success."

I fiddled with my fingers while taking in what she said. "How does it work exactly?"

"Well, when a candidate, let's say you for example, decides to join the auction, there is a list of rules and requirements that must be met. The primary ones are as follows:

You must marry the bidder within thirty days of signing the contract the night of the auction.

You must consummate that marriage within two weeks of the wedding ceremony.

You must live, travel, and have regular sexual relations as any married couple would, for a period of three years."

"And what happens after the three-year period?" I interrupted.

"That is up to you and your husband. Most of my matches end up falling in love and staying together."

"And if I agreed to marry a stranger?" I gulped then let out a sharp breath. "God, I can't believe those words just came out of my mouth. My mother would freakin' kill me." I released a nervous sigh. "If I agreed to marry some rich guy, I'd get three million dollars?"

"Most of my candidates go for far more. A beauty like you…" She tapped her crimson nail against her perfectly matching red lips as she hummed then tilted her head while accessing my face. "If I had to guess, which I despise doing *chérie*, because truly you are priceless in your own way…"

"But if you had to guess?" I encouraged.

"No less than five million."

"Ho, ho, ho, Merry Frickin' Christmas to me! Jesus," I blurted and covered my face with both of my hands. "Five million dollars. I can't even imagine having that much money. It would be life changing. Heck, it would change my entire family's lives. My parents could retire comfortably, and I could open my bar."

"Exactly. And possibly gain yourself a true partner in life," Alana added, as if that mattered even a little bit.

"Pssshhhhttt!" I waved her off. "I've dated a lot of men. All of them left much to be desired. I'm perfectly happy being alone and a spinster."

"You do not wish for love, *chérie?*" Alana did that thing where she covered her heart with her hand. I was beginning to hate that gesture. It seemed everyone around me felt the need to protect their heart.

Maybe I'd become too cynical, but I'd never in my thirty years of life met a man I loved enough to even want to get married. Sharing my entire existence with someone and having my happiness all wrapped up in theirs sounded like the cherry on a shit cake. I guess I was too selfish for that.

Personally, I wanted a thriving business of my own making. I wanted to be the one to secure my future happiness. However, the one thing I did miss about being in a committed relationship was regular sex. It had been a solid year since my last hook-up, and the Lord knew I could use a wild romp in the sack.

"No, I don't wish for love. I have love in my life. My

parents, my friends, Mac and his club downstairs. Love doesn't have to be romantic in order to feel fulfilled. At least not to me it doesn't," I stated emphatically.

It drove me up the wall when people thought my life wasn't full because it didn't have a man in it. Not that Alana suggested that specifically, but the underlying point had to be made. I wasn't lacking anything because I didn't have a man. I was lacking a heaping pile of cash to make all my dreams come true, not a guy.

Alana's smile turned positively wicked. "Then it seems I have chosen well. You want financial security. I can give you that. It just depends on whether or not you are willing to give up your freedom, and the life you currently live, for the next three years in order to get it."

"What's in it for them? Better yet, what's in it for you? Do you get a cut of my three mil?"

She shook her head. "My commission gets paid by the bidder. You pay nothing. On the night of the auction, once you both sign on the dotted line, you are sent a deposit of $250,000. Once you are married a third of the bid gets transferred. Then on your first anniversary the second installment, and the same on the next anniversary. By the third anniversary if you do not want to stay married, you get divorced."

I sucked air through my teeth as I considered that once I got married to my bidder, I'd be a million dollars richer. That was a *lot* of money.

"And what happens if the bidder doesn't like what he purchases or I can't stand him?"

Alana smiled. "There are systems in place for that as well. That is why we suggest the wedding occur within thirty days of the auction, so you have time to get to know your husband. However, I am doing something entirely different for the Christmas auction. For the next month, I have requested each bidder take the candidate they are interested in on a date."

"A date?"

"*Oui*. This will give the candidate and the bidder a bit of time to connect. See if there is physical attraction, camaraderie, shared interests, maybe even an insta-love connection."

I snort-laughed and received a raised eyebrow from Alana in response. "Do you mock me?"

"No, God no!" I rushed to explain. "I just think insta-love is only in fairytales. Insta-lust sure. I've experienced that a time, or *ten*. But I've never believed in that love-at-first-sight stuff. It's impractical and unrealistic, in my humble opinion. But you know, my mom always taught me, 'to each their own.' Just because I haven't experienced it, doesn't mean it doesn't exist."

"I agree," Alana said.

"Um, now about the bidders. What's in it for them?"

"Each bidder has their own reasons. I've heard and seen it all."

"Could you be more specific? If I'm to consider a monster-sized risk, marriage to a stranger, I need to see this plan from both sides."

Alana tapped her nail on the table and pursed her lips. "I cannot give you names or likenesses, but I can share some scenarios, if that would help."

"It would. It totally would." I smiled and danced in my chair encouragingly.

"Well let's see, I've had twin brothers who were set to gain an enormous inheritance provided they were married. Another was hopelessly in love with a woman that had put herself up for auction in order to gain enough money to save her family's land from being purchased from underneath her, by that same man in fact."

"No way! That's scandalous as all get-out. What happened?" I leaned forward, hoping to pull the details from her faster.

"They got married, fell in love, and are expanding their

family."

"Wow. I'll bet that match made you feel like a boss bitch." I chuckled.

She smirked. "Truth be told, I'm rather proud of that pairing."

"What else?"

"Sometimes it's not so exciting. One male candidate I had needed a great deal of money to help his very large family. The woman who purchased him had given up on the idea of love and just wanted a man in her life to be there for her. Another bidder was lonely and a single father who had been widowed. Let's see… Oh, the last auction, I had a bidder who wanted to find a woman he could love and have children with."

"Children?" I scoffed. "You mean some of these matches have babies even knowing they're going to end their marriage in three years?"

Alana nodded. "Everything is up for negotiation."

"Would I be required to have a child? Because if that's the case, I'm out. There's no amount of money that could make me want to have a baby with a stranger. I'm not even sure I want kids."

Alana laughed. "No, no, *chérie*. Once you've agreed to participate, we go through all of your likes and dislikes, sexually and otherwise. We are professionals in setting up marriages of convenience, not baby breeders. However, some couples enter into the auction to find a forever pairing. Some actually want children regardless of the time limit. If both parties are open to such thing, we make that known in the contract."

"Well, put me down for the 'no baby' option," I said dryly. I couldn't even imagine such a thing.

"Does that mean you are open to entering the auction? I'm afraid I do need an answer rather quickly as we have already entered into our one-month window of setting up dates with potential bidders prior to the actual auction on Christmas Eve."

"I don't know," I worried my bottom lip with my teeth. "I need to think about it. Can I have a couple days?"

Alana nodded, grabbed her wristlet and pulled out another of those black business cards. Her name was on one side, a phone number on the other. That was it. So cool. She slid the card across the table and stood up.

"I hope to hear from you, Holly. I do believe you'd be the perfect candidate for this event. Think about it. And if you have any additional questions, feel free to call." She pointed at the door to my apartment. "I'll see myself out."

"Uh, yeah," I stood up feeling a little shaky. "Thank you for…um…thinking of me. I'll consider it."

"You do that. *Au revoir.*"

Alana left through the door, and I slumped back into my kitchen chair, holding her card. *Am I seriously considering this?* Three million for three years. Marrying a stranger. It seemed completely unreal. Like I'd entered one of those parallel universe movies. Then again, the money was nothing to sneeze at. And it was only three years.

My mind swam with visions of the establishment I wanted to open. The handcrafted mahogany bar I'd have made, the colorful bottles of top shelf liquor I'd stock. The super unique glasses and different drinks I'd offer. I had a journal of all the ideas I had for Night Owl, the name I'd chosen for my dream bar. I'd planned to make the inside look uber chic yet earthy like being inside a dark, dreamy forest. I'd even sketched an owl with little stars around it as the potential logo.

The more I thought about my dream bar, the more I considered accepting the opportunity Alana had presented. Yet the big question swirling like a vortex within my mind was the same.

Could I marry a stranger for a boatload of money?

Chapter 5

Two Turtledoves

BRUNO

"You're a dead man, Joel," I threatened. I paced the conference room, glancing out at Sin City through the floor-to-ceiling windows while I pressed my cell phone closer to my ear.

"What did I do this time?" Joel chuckled, his voice sounding gruff through the phone.

"You pretty much demanded I take this Marriage Auction contract, and here I am, waiting to meet the next candidate I will be guarding through a week of first dates with a bunch of rich pricks."

"Oh, come on, it can't be that bad," Joel countered and then coughed.

I hissed through my teeth. "You should hear the lame shit these men say to the women. And worse is how the women respond as though they adore every breath of air escaping the blowhards' mouths."

Joel chuckled. "Like what? I'm intrigued."

I groaned. "Well, the last date I went on the bidder took the candidate to a zoo. When they stopped to watch the lion habitat, a pair of lions were fornicating. The guy pointed it out then made a joke to the candidate about how he'd like to be doing that with her."

"I'm beginning to see your point," Joel grumbled and then coughed again.

"You have a cold?"

"I'm trying not to have one. Penny came home with one from elementary school and now Faith, Eden, and I are all starting to feel the effects."

"Another reason not to have children," I taunted.

"Children are the best, Bruno. Don't knock it until you've tried it."

That made me chuckle. "Yeah, I don't think it's in the cards for me. I'll leave all that legacy and progeny business to you, cousin."

Joel sighed. "I do wish you'd at least find someone special to share your free time with."

"Free time? What free time? And Joel, we've talked about—"

"This before. Yes, I know. It doesn't change the fact that you are a thirty-four-year-old man with nothing but work in his life. Believe me when I say there is more. You know I thought I'd lost all hope for happiness when Alexandra died and left me to raise Penny alone. Seeing Faith standing up on that stage in the auction last year changed my entire life. And look at me now. Happier than I've ever been."

"I'm not like you, Joel. You make time for those you love. I've not met anyone that made me want to slow down. My work is my life. Besides, I wouldn't want a woman who didn't understand that. My career matters to me."

"But what about love? What about sex?"

"Sex I can get. And if you count up all the so-called dates I've been on, not a single woman has ever made me feel anything but lust." Truth be told, I wouldn't even begin to know what love feels like as I've never experienced it before.

"That's because your father, Uncle Nicko, was a womanizing piece of shit. Your mother deserved better, Bruno."

"On that we both agree, God rest her soul."

"God rest her soul," Joel croaked, his voice losing its pitch all together.

"Joel, why don't you find that beautiful wife of yours and make both of you some tea and then go back to bed? You sound terrible."

"Yeah, I'm thinking movie day in with the girls." He sighed. "Just give the experience a chance. You never know, maybe the woman of your dreams will be standing on that stage, looking into your eyes, and you'll just know she's the one."

"Doubtful, but I promise to relax. The job is easy. After everything that's happened within the last year, I sure could use an easy job."

"There you go. See, you're already taking a more positive slant to the approach. Oh, whatever happened to that woman you saved a few days ago? Is she okay?"

Visions of Holly entered my mind. Her long, wavy blonde hair, those warm brown eyes, the cute beauty mark just above her plump, full lips. My cock started to harden behind my slacks, shocking me stupid for a moment.

"Was she released from the hospital?" Joel asked.

I attempted to shake off the lust, even though my lower half was taking its sweet time getting the message from my brain.

"Uh, yeah, she was. The next day. Apparently, Alana went to see her a couple days ago. Offered her a coveted position in this year's Christmas auction. I'm still waiting to hear if she's accepted or not." A strange part of me didn't want to believe that Holly would entertain such a ridiculous concept. The woman seemed self-assured, confident, and very much her own person. I especially didn't want to see her bowing down to some rich pencil dick.

"Don't be surprised if she does join. Alana has a way of getting others to do things they wouldn't do otherwise."

"Isn't that the truth. I'm a perfect example." I laughed out loud then heard the door behind me open. I turned around and was shocked to see the woman herself, dressed in a pair of skintight black jeans, suede ankle boots, a slouchy white sweater that hung off one tanned shoulder and a lion's mane of golden hair.

"It's you!" Holly exclaimed with a huge smile plastered on her face as Alana entered behind her.

"I gotta go, Joel. Christmas came early. Remember, lots of fluids and rest."

"Yeah, ye—" He coughed for the umpteenth time. "Good luck."

"Thanks, I'm going to need it." I ended the call and dropped the device into my blazer pocket. "How are you feeling, Holly?" I took the chair next to the blonde beauty.

"So good. I'm pretty much all healed up." She showed me the abrasions on her palms that were all scabbed over. There were still fingerprint shaped yellow bruises around her neck that sent fire blazing through my core. Instantly, I wanted to pound my fists repeatedly into the Baskin brothers once more. Thankfully, I'd had Jonah keep an eye on their status. Both men were firmly locked away in the local jail until sentencing. I'd be the first in line to serve as a witness on the criminal case, provided they didn't take a plea and it went to trial.

"That's very good to hear. And you're joining us today because…" I let the rest of the question dangle, hoping I was not about to hear what I feared most.

"I'm joining the Christmas Auction. I'm going to get shacked up for an obscene amount of money and open my bar when it's all said and done three years from now," Holly beamed.

I couldn't believe the unexpected burst of anger that flooded my system. I pushed away from the conference table and stood up. "Seriously?" I barked, my gaze going straight to Alana. "Hasn't Holly been through enough?"

Alana sat up straighter, then eased back into the leather chair and primly placed her hands together in her lap. "Are you suggesting that the auction isn't safe? I do believe that is why you are here, Mr. Castellanos. To keep my candidates perfectly safe, is it not?"

"Yes," I hissed.

"Do you not think I'd be a good candidate?" Holly blurted, a hurt note to her voice.

"No! I mean, yes. Fuck!" I snapped and ran my fingers through my hair. I focused my gaze outside on the busy streets and the tourists walking from one casino to the other. "I'm sure you'd make some man very happy, but after what you went through…"

"After what I went through?" Holly parroted. "The reason I said yes is because of what happened. I can't be in that situation anymore, where I'm running an out of-the-way bar, saving every penny, and still having no life while I get no closer to my dreams. What Alana has offered is going to set me up for the foreseeable future. I'm not sure you can understand that," she whispered and put her head down as I turned around.

"I can very much understand being raised poor and having to fight for every dollar I've ever made. That's why I own my company and hire only the best."

"You see, I want that for myself one day. If I go through with marrying a man this month, then I'll have the money I need to do exactly that."

"And what if you fall in love with your husband? Then what about your big dreams?" I spat in a snide tone I didn't even recognize. "They just go the way of the wind?"

What the fuck was wrong with me? I was entirely riled up by the idea of this woman getting married to a complete stranger, and I had no idea why. Was it because I'd helped save her life? Or maybe it was because I was once like her and didn't want her dreams steamrolled by someone else's plans.

She shook her head and glared at me. "My big dreams have nothing to do with marriage and love. And besides, if the man I end up with doesn't care for me enough to want to see me succeed and help make my dreams come true, then I'd be a fool to stay with him, wouldn't I? And another thing, Mr. Know-It-All, I'm going into this scenario with my eyes wide open. I tried other avenues for securing the financial support I needed. This is the only option left."

It was on the tip of my tongue to offer her the money she needed, but that would be ludicrous. I'd essentially known the woman for mere hours if I added up all the time we'd been in the same space together. Not to mention, the fury in her gaze and the ire in Alana's had me believing that making such an offer would not be well received.

I inhaled deeply and let it out slowly, desperately trying to calm my own frayed nerves.

"Whatever. It's your life," I snapped through clenched teeth.

"You're damn right it is. And I don't need you or anyone else telling me what to do. I have parents who love to do that already." She nodded as though she'd given me some kind of what-for. It was cute that this precious woman thought this conversation was over. I just needed more time to change her mind and help her find another way.

But why the fuck did I even care?

"Well, now that we've got all of that out of the way," Alana interrupted, "I brought Holly in to explain to you both that you will be working together for the duration of this auction. Apparently, you've been rather forthright with your feelings on the marriage auction with the other candidate you guarded this week." Her gaze turned into a glare. "Lisa no longer wants you as her guard. She feels as though you are a deterrent to her finding her best match."

"A deterrent? That last guy would have had his hands all over her if I hadn't pushed him away."

"According to Lisa, and my bidder, you bent back his pinky finger, almost breaking it, when he tried to guide her into the limo after their dinner."

"Pfft. This is unbelievable. He's lying. I purposely sprained the man's pinky finger when he went to grab her ass, without her consent I might add, after repeatedly telling her he couldn't wait to bid on her, so he could fuck her into next week."

Alana's eyes widened for a brief second. "My apologies. I shall instead thank you for intervening. However, you could have reminded the bidder that touching intimately is off limits. You didn't need to resort to violence."

"Spraining his finger is not violence," I deadpanned. "The atrocity that Holly experienced last week was violence. Me beating his face to a bloody pulp like I wanted to, like I did do to one of the Baskin brothers, would be considered violent."

"Be that as it may, Mr. Castellanos, I'd like to see you refrain from your baser instincts when possible. Use your words, not your fists, unless you believe the situation is dire."

"Now you're telling me how to do my job?" I grinned then allowed myself a full-throated laugh.

"I'm paying you handsomely to guard my candidates, not to threaten or maim my bidders." She cocked a saucy black eyebrow.

"Well, if your bidders had better manners, perhaps we

wouldn't be having this discussion in the first place."

Alana pursed her lips. "*Touché.* I will have my protégé, Jade, send out a reminder to all candidates and bidders about what type of conduct is appropriate for our dates prior to the auction. Usually, we just have the auction with no prior contact. This is new territory for me, and we are learning as we go. I appreciate your candor and will take your feedback to heart. Is that acceptable?"

Damn, the woman was good. Within a short conversation she's already dampened my anger with her annoyingly reasonable response.

"Yes," I grated.

"Excellent." She smiled. "Let's continue." She swiped her fingers over an electronic tablet. "Holly's first date is with Colin Omstead—"

"The actor!" Holly gasped. "Colin Omstead, the guy that played in *Drifter 1, 2,* and *3!*" she half-screeched. "Oh my god! Are you shitting me?"

"I do not understand this American colloquialism *shitting me, chérie,* but my guess is you are asking if I am being truthful?" Alana queried.

"Um, yeah. Am I really going to go on a date with stud muffin Colin Omstead?" She started to dance in her chair like a tween about to meet her favorite Hollywood crush.

Alana smiled wide. "I see you like the idea of this pairing."

"Hell yeah, I do! Sign me up! Not in a million years did I believe I'd be going on a date with one of the hottest action flick actors of all time. You should have led with that when pitching the idea of the auction, and I would have agreed the same night you made the offer."

"Duly noted for future negotiations," Alana preened. "I am elated you are excited. The date is slated for tomorrow evening. We will have you go through the entire makeover and clothing fitting today and tomorrow morning, if that is agreeable."

"You're going to give me a makeover too? And I don't have to pay for it?" She pulled on her gorgeous locks, twirling a chunk around her finger absently.

I couldn't help staring at her. Holly Knight was uniquely beautiful, but it was her mannerisms that I enjoyed watching most. The woman didn't pretend or play games. She reacted and responded naturally and with gusto, whereas the other candidates I met were more shy, quiet, and seemed content to observe, rather than participate. It was refreshing to meet a woman who was herself so openly.

Alana smiled and noted something on her device. "Everything is set. If you'll follow me, Holly, I'll take you to meet your glam team."

"I have a glam team?" she breathed, clearly awed.

I rolled my eyes and clamped my mouth shut.

"Only the best for my candidates and bidders as promised. Now, let's see if we can pick out an outfit that will have Mr. Omstead drooling to bid on you."

"Fucking hell," I grumbled under my breath. I hated the idea that a woman like Holly was going to be a part of this.

"What was that Mr. Castellanos? I didn't quite hear you." Alana had cocked one eyebrow as her gaze narrowed with the question.

"Lead the way. I'll just be keeping an eye on my girl."

Alana canted her head to the side as I realized what I'd just said.

"I mean, *your*…candidate."

"That is what I thought you said. Come, Holly. A man like Colin Omstead will be a perfect pairing. Two turtledoves finding one another," she cooed.

On that note, I clenched my teeth and followed the two women, hating every last second of watching Holly prepare to be wooed by another man.

I needed a fucking drink.

Chapter 6

A Christmas Affair

HOLLY

The hairstylist just finished giving me a fresh haircut, blowout, and style. My hair had never looked shiner or healthier.

"Wow, you are an artist," I gushed while fluffing my hair on either side. I glanced at the grumpy brooding man sitting not ten feet away.

"I know," Henrietta agreed with zero humility and a saucy purse of her lips.

Henrietta was a stunning trans woman who confided that she used to go by the name Henry, after I mentioned I'd never met a Henrietta before. Apparently, her momma was none too happy that there would be a name change along with her child's transition. And not because she had a problem with her child's choice to identify as a woman. That actually did not factor in her mother's reaction at all. It had everything to do with the fact that Henrietta's grandfather was named Henry, and mom wanted to keep the name in the family. Together, they came up with Henrietta, because it was closest to the grandfather's name, and it also felt more genuine to Henrietta in her transition. I found this all incredibly sweet and hilarious, because when she told the story, she acted each person out with hand movements and gestures to boot—a one-person stage show.

She played with my hair and smiled wide. "Alana scooped me up and added me to her glam team when I filled in for one of her regulars. It's been true love and beauty between us ever since. Right, Big A?" she hollered loud enough for Alana to hear where she stood across the room going through a rack of extraordinary designer dresses.

"Of course, *ma petite fleur*. When I see a unique talent such as yours, I must have it for my team," Alana confirmed without taking her eyes off the clothing. "This is *magnifique!*" Alana gasped. "Holly, what do you think?"

I turned my head, and my mouth dropped open. It was my favorite color, forest green and made entirely out of beads and sequins. The dress had spaghetti straps and a heart-shaped neckline that would make my girls look fabulous. The top was interspersed with beads, sequins, and illusion mesh, making it ultra-sexy. The bottom was draped with fabric sequins all the way to the floor that came together at the hip where a daring slit pulled away.

It was phenomenal.

"Holy shit, Alana," I breathed then popped out of the stylist chair and dashed to her side. I touched and petted the dress as though it were a living breathing thing. And after I saw the $10,000 price tag, I was sure I'd have to feed and water the damn thing before touching it again.

"She can't wear that," Bruno announced at the same time I said, "I can't wear that."

Alana looked at Bruno with daggers in her gaze before it softened when she addressed me. "Do you not like it, *chérie?*"

I shook my head repeatedly. "No, I do." I reached out but thought better of it and dropped my hand to my side. I'd never owned anything that expensive outside of my car and even that was a hand-me-down my dad gave me when they upgraded one of their cars several years ago. "I mean, it's beautiful, but far too expensive."

"Not to mention completely *inappropriate* for a first date," Bruno grumbled.

I spun around and braced my hands to my hips and glared at the man. "Is this how you're going to be all the time? Opinionated and combative? Because if you are, I have no problem requesting a new guard like that other candidate did. Just because you saved my life doesn't mean you get to dictate how I live it."

Bruno's jaw flexed and his lips twisted into a snarl. "Duly noted. I apologize. I just meant that it's rather revealing and—"

"Pssshttt!" I snorted. "Revealing is the point, is it not, Alana? The bidders need a sample of the merchandise. I know I would want to see the goods before I paid millions for something."

Alana smiled. "I'm glad you feel that way, Holly, because as a reminder, at the auction, we have a lingerie portion where you will be wearing very little."

"Makes sense," I said at the same time Bruno said, "The fuck you are!"

Once again, I rounded on Bruno, but this time I stomped over to him and stood toe-to-toe. He was a solid six inches taller than my five feet eight inches, but that didn't deter me in the least. Fire raced down my spine as my frustration boiled over.

I pointed right at his chest with purpose. "What did I say not ten seconds ago, Mister Grumpy Pants? You do not get to dictate what I do with my life. And why are you bothering anyway?"

He raised his hands and backed up a few steps, shaking his head. "Jesus, Holly, I'm sorry. Truly I am. It is not my place. I think you three have this covered. I don't need to be here for this. I'm going to check in with my team. I'll be in the conference room when you're ready to leave," he spouted and took off.

My shoulders fell, and the anger dissipated while my frustration still simmered. "What the heck has that guy's panties in a twist?" I huffed and made my way back to Alana.

"God, it's so obvious, girl," Henrietta smacked her lips as she applied new gloss.

"What is?"

"That man is into you," she said.

I frowned and gnawed on my bottom lip. "What are you talking about?"

Henrietta smirked but didn't say anything, so I focused my attention on Alana. "Any help here?"

Alana simply smiled.

"Oh, for heaven's sake child," Henrietta blurted. "He likes you. So much so that he doesn't want any man seeing you in that hot-as-fuck dress, or prancing around the auction in your skivvies."

I waved my hand at Henrietta. "Puh-leeze. Bruno's given me no indication he likes me. As a matter of fact, I'd have suspected the opposite if he didn't save me a few days ago." I shook my head. "Ya know, that's probably what it is. He feels responsible for me somehow. Alana, what do you think?"

Alana batted her eyelashes and shrugged her shoulder with visible nonchalance. "I do not know one way or the other. Perhaps you should discuss it with him tonight in your shared suite."

"Shared suite? You mean I'm rooming with him?"

Dread, thick as molasses, filled my gut. If Bruno was already mad—and I had no clue why he would be so upset—I'd chosen to participate in the auction, living with him for the next three weeks was going to be the pits. But no way would I complain; I was being offered an opportunity of a lifetime.

Alana narrowed her eyes. "Darling, I cannot keep you protected if he's not sharing the same space. However, you have your own rooms with a living space separating them. Is that not acceptable?" she cooed.

"Uh, no, it's…um…fine. I'll make it work. How's about we change the subject and I try on that dress?"

"Fabulous!" Alana beamed as she passed the gorgeous dress to me. "There's a privacy screen over there you can use."

"Awesome," I said and took the dress behind the screen. "So, what's this date tomorrow going to be like? Do they tell you in advance?" I shucked my clothes into a pile on the floor and stared at the most incredible dress I'd ever seen hanging before me. It stole my breath it was so beautiful. Reminded me of something a Hollywood starlet would wear, not a bartender from Las Vegas.

"*Oui,* chérie. We are informed of every detail. Colin is taking you to an industry charity event and silent auction in Los Angeles. Very luxe. Many celebrities will be in attendance. It's red carpet so the dress needs to be fashionable and expensive. Alas, you needn't worry about a thing. The price of this dress, your shoes, jewelry and everything included for the trip comes out of Mr. Omstead's expenses. He chose the event and set the expectation specifically for the type of woman he wanted to have on his arm. You fit the request perfectly."

"I'm going to Los Angeles tomorrow. As in, California?" I squealed as I pulled the dress up my body and stood as high up on tiptoe as possible so I wouldn't drag the fabric along the ground.

Both Alana and Henrietta gasped at the sight of me in the dress when I came around the partition.

"You look like a Christmas present ready to be unwrapped,

sister!" Henrietta exclaimed.

"Oh *chérie*, you are too beautiful for words. This dress was made for you," Alana added.

I tiptoed over to the full-length mirror and inspected myself. I didn't recognize the elegant woman standing before me. She was me, but not. She was the me I knew deep down in my soul I could be.

"It's perfect. I feel like a million dollars." I turned from side to side inspecting it from every angle, especially the daring open back. The dress showed everything and nothing at the same time.

Alana approached and gently grasped my arms on either side from behind. We both stared at my reflection in the mirror.

"It will be a Christmas affair to remember, my darling. Take it all in, Holly, because your entire life is about to change."

Chapter 7

Rudolph the Red Nosed Reindeer

BRUNO

"What the fuck is wrong with me?" I hissed as I slammed the conference room door.

I walked over to the table, pressed my palms to the wooden surface and braced myself as I sucked in several deep breaths. My usual nerves of steel were completely *rattled*. I'd spent years on a battlefield without so much as a twitch in the middle of combat, but the idea of Holly parading around in lingerie in a room full of strangers like some sex kitten set me off.

Why?

Holly was my charge, *not* my girlfriend.

I huffed at the thought of her being my girlfriend. I hadn't had a girlfriend in longer than I could remember. Maybe I just needed to get laid. It had been a few weeks since my last hookup. That's all it was. I needed to wet the whistle, clean out the pipes, and take the edge off. I'm sure that's all it was…right?

My phone buzzed in my pocket. The display said it was Jonas, my second, calling.

"Yeah," I grunted into the phone, still thinking about Holly and the fool I'd made of myself not only in front of her, but a fucking client.

"You asked me to check out a guy named Colin Omstead," Jonas reminded.

"What've you got?" I turned around and sat on the edge of the table, content to disappear into work versus my muddled thoughts of a blonde I had no business imagining in her lingerie.

"Omstead is an American actor. Beloved by his fans, most specifically of the female variety."

"Yeah, I'll just bet he is." *Fucker.* "And?"

"Worth about two hundred million. Thirty-five. No police record. Received a few awards in acting over the years. Has a BA from UCLA. Donates ten percent of his income to charity each year…"

"For fuck sake. Is the man a saint?"

Jonas chuckled. "Seems like it, man. I haven't found a single skeleton in his closet. He not only looks good on paper, he's on *People* magazine's list of most eligible bachelors and often referred to by the media as, 'the man with the gilded chest,' because he looks like an Adonis. He's clean."

I rubbed at my temples with my thumb and forefinger. "So he's perfect," I grumbled.

"For bidding on a wife in Ms. Toussaint's auction, yeah. Why did you have me run him a second time?" Jonah pushed. I knew he would ask. I never had him run things twice. If he did the job, I knew straight to my bones he'd do it right the first time, every time. Because in our line of work, people died if mistakes were made, and we'd learned that lesson the hard way.

Jonas was like a brother to me. Not by blood, but through sacrifice. We'd survived some serious shit together in special ops and when we finally got out alive, he was one of two people in the world I trusted.

"Honestly?"

"Always man, you know you can unload on me."

I let out a long breath. "I don't know, Jonas. There's something about Holly being a part of this charade that's getting under my skin."

"Do you think it's the fact that you saved her life, so you feel protective over her?" His tone was exploratory.

"Maybe."

"Are you attracted to her?"

"You've seen her picture, Jonas."

He laughed out loud, the sound easing the tension in my chest a bit. There was a time Jonas didn't laugh. Years of time, in fact. To hear it now proved how far we'd come.

"Maybe you just want to fuck her and you're feeling territorial. It's not your normal MO, brother, but that woman is your type, man."

"I don't have a type," I snapped.

"Bullshit! The last five women you had me do background checks on before you fucked were blonde, tall, with a banging body. You can't lie to me. I know you better than you know yourself, you broody bastard."

I growled under my breath. "Then what should I do about it?"

"Ignore it. She's off limits, Bruno. She's spoken for. When she's settled in for the evening, put one of our men at the door and hit the casino. Find yourself another blonde that strikes your fancy and have a night of good old-fashioned, consensual fun with a lady that wants the same."

That made me chuckle. "Consensual fun. Put down the self-help books, brother." I went over to the window and watched the sun slip behind the horizon. One thing about Las Vegas, the desert was beautiful.

"You know the new saying, right? Consent is sexy."

"I have never, and will never, have sex with an unwilling woman. Of course consent is necessary," I blurted.

A throat cleared from behind me.

Alana and Holly stood staring, one with eyes widened in surprise, the other having clamped her hand over mouth to staunch her laughter.

I let my head drop back and glared at the ceiling. "Thank you for the enlightening conversation, Jonas. I'll touch base tomorrow," I sighed and abruptly ended the call and the sound of his laughter.

"Holly is ready to settle in for the night," Alana stated, her hands clasped together in front of her, the model of cool, calm, and collected.

"Perfect. Let's go." I said, gesturing to the door and the elevators down the hall.

Alana broke off at the hallway leading to her office. "Mr. Castellanos, Holly will need to be back here at ten a.m. Mr. Omstead's private jet leaves at two and we'll want plenty of time with her glam team to prepare for her date. You will escort her everywhere but keep your distance as to not intrude on their affair."

"I know how to do my job, Alana. And feel free to call me Bruno. We've known one another for quite some time now."

She dipped her chin primly. *"Fais de beaux rêves, ma chérie."*

The door to the elevator opened and I urged Holly inside with my hand on her lower back.

"Bye! Thank you!" She waved then pouted. "I don't know what she said."

"She said, 'sweet dreams, dear.'" I explained.

"You speak French?" Her big brown eyes widened in awe, the colors swirling like heated caramel.

"I speak many languages."

"Wow. That's cool. How do you say, thank you so much, in French?" she asked.

"*Merci beaucoup*," I translated.

"*Merci beaucoup*," she repeated. "And in Spanish?"

"*Muchas gracias*." I clenched my teeth in order not to smile. The woman was not only gorgeous, but adorable.

"How about German?" her expression shifted to one of wonder.

"*Danke sehr*."

"Awesome. How's about…umm, Italian!" she blurted as though she'd stump me.

"*Grazie mille*," I smirked and cocked an eyebrow, wondering what she'd come up with next.

"Ohhhh I know! I'm gonna get you on this one," she pressed. "Japanese!"

"*Dōmo arigatō gozaimasu*." I put my hands together and bowed forward.

She started to bounce on her feet, enjoying this game. The doors opened to one of the upper floors that held the luxury suites.

"What about…Norwegian!" she said happily as we passed by one of my guards. I nodded in greeting, and he did the same.

My men were dotted throughout the floor, strategically placed, and perfectly poised, as expected from a member of my team. I paid my men very well. They trained for boredom, torture, high stress environments and everything in between. If you wanted a job done right, you hired my company. My men were an extension of what Jonas and I built from the ground up. All former military special operators. There was no better security service in the world.

"*Tusen takk*," I murmured as we made it to our suite.

I opened the door and watched as Holly's mouth dropped open at the sheer opulence of the suite. Alana did not scrimp, that's for sure.

"Holy shit! Have you ever seen anything so beautiful?" She spun around, her arms open wide, her booted feet clicking on the tile as she did so. Her golden hair fanned out around her shoulders when she stopped. Her cheeks were pink, and her eyes glittered with excitement.

"No, I haven't," I whispered, not looking anywhere but at her.

She swallowed as our gazes met, her chest rising and falling with her labored breaths. Her nipples peaked against the fabric as she licked her plump lips so sensually, I could almost taste her sweet berry flavor on the very air between us. I wanted to rip her sweater down the center and put my hands all over rounded curves.

Instead, I fisted my hands and offered a fake smile. "I need a drink."

Her eyes lit up. "Ohhh, me too! Do you think they'll charge an arm and a leg for it?"

I closed my eyes, allowing a renewed sense of patience and control to take over. "It doesn't matter, Holly. Everything from the second you arrived to the moment you sign the marriage contract is free of charge. Live it up."

"Very nice. I'm gonna order room service too. But first, I'm going to change. Will you make me a drink?" she asked as she located the room where her luggage could be clearly seen in one of the two king-sized bedrooms. I knew this because my men had already done recon prior to our arrival. Usually, I would check every nook and cranny prior to allowing my charge to enter to be certain it was safe, but it wasn't necessary when my guys were on the job.

"What do you want?" I called out and headed to the bar.

"Anything with whiskey in it," she hollered.

I pulled out a bottle of Glenlivet and poured us both a glass with two fingers. I slammed the first, appreciating the heat as it raced down my throat and filled my gut, then poured myself another. I'd need the liquid courage to get through a night of forced proximity.

Within what felt like mere minutes Holly was sauntering through the room bare footed wearing Christmas pajamas.

I scoffed at the sight. "What the fuck are you wearing?"

She frowned and looked down at the satin shorts and matching button-up, short-sleeved top that had a bunch of leaping cartoon deer with round red noses imprinted all over them. It was hard to focus on any one of them since the pattern was complete chaos.

Holly shimmied from one side to the other as though showing them off. "Aren't they cute! It's Rudolph the Red Nosed Reindeer. They're hilarious and comfy." She beamed.

I shook my head and handed her the drink.

"What? Does Mr. Grumpy Pants not like Rudolph?" She waggled her brows and sipped at her drink. "Needs soda," she murmured and went over to the bar, found a can of Coke and poured it to the top.

"If you wanted a whiskey and Coke, you should've just asked for one."

She shrugged. "I didn't know I wanted it until I got the drink and tasted it. Sometimes one doesn't realize what they want until they've already had the same ole thing. Kinda like this auction."

"How so?" I tilted my head and leaned against the back of the couch.

She went around me and plopped on the seat and pulled her long, tanned legs, up and to the side, resting most of her weight on her hip.

"Well, I never thought much about getting married before. Ever since I was a little girl, I dreamed of owning my own business and making a ton of money. Traveling the world, taking lavish vacations. Marriage and kids never really factored into it. Now that I'm entering the auction, I'm going to be married and well off. And at the end of that three-year period, I'll be opening my own bar."

This was fascinating information. "What if you fall in love with your husband?"

She shrugged. "Like I said before. If my husband and I end up falling in love, then he'll have to understand that I'm going to make my dreams a reality. I don't plan to arrange my life or cater to his needs alone. That's not a marriage."

"And if he travels constantly for work? What then?"

"Lots of couples are happy in relationships where they don't see their partner every day. If he was living his dream while I was living mine, I'm sure we could find a happy medium so that we could make time for one another."

"Interesting." I said and then went around the couch and took a seat, shucking off my shoes and putting my socked feet up onto the table. "So you're saying, if your husband worked say, two weeks out of every month, you'd be okay with that?"

She nodded. "Of course. I'm not the type of girl that would sit around and pine after my man. If he was my man, I'd miss him, but there are things called phones and video calls." She drank a large portion of her drink. "And just think, the phone sex would be off the chain, not to mention the fun it would be when he came home. Honestly, I couldn't imagine a better scenario." She leaned back, closed her eyes, probably imagining it right now. "My prince charming, surprising me at my very own bar, whisking me away to the back room for a hot shag on my office desk...*yummy*," she hummed seductively.

My cock heard that low hum and paid close attention, hardening behind my slacks while my mind gave that salacious vision a whirl.

"Can you imagine it?" She opened her eyes, her pupils dilated, her mouth slightly open.

Lust filled the air between us. It took everything in me not to groan and kneel before her and take her mouth in a searing kiss. I would be willing to bet she tasted like ripened fruit. Succulent and dripping with sweetness.

I cleared my throat and downed another gulp of my whiskey, needing the burn to wash away my insanity. "Yeah, you set the scene perfectly," I grated and stood, hiding my erection by turning away from her. "I'm going to order dinner and then take a shower." A fucking cold one. "What do you want?"

"What are you getting?"

"Steak, potato, veg," I grumbled.

"Make that dinner for two and add a slice of chocolate cake! I'll unpack while you do your thing."

Oh, I'll be doing my thing all right, with my hand wrapped around my cock, imagining her bent over the back of that couch while Rudolph stares me down with every thrust.

Fucking hell, I did need to get laid.

After ordering the food, I rubbed my hand down my face and disappeared into my bedroom. I left the door open a crack, the same as the bathroom door, to ensure I could hear her in case she needed me.

I turned on the shower as I shucked off my clothes and stepped under the spray.

Visions of her wiggling out of her reindeer pajamas and presenting me with her juicy ass had me circling my cock with my hand.

"Fucking Rudolph," I groaned as I stroked, tipping my head back and enjoying the moment.

Chapter 8

Christmas Came *Early*

HOLLY

Our food arrived seemingly at the speed of light. I let the hotel attendant bring the cart in and set the dining table for two, instructing him to leave the metal food warmers over the plates to keep the food hot. And since I wasn't paying for anything, I gave the man a fat twenty-five percent tip.

I lifted one of the domes and allowed the scent of the steak to waft in the air. My mouth watered and my belly rumbled as I covered it once more. When I glanced at Bruno's room, I noticed he'd left the door open. That probably meant he was open to me interrupting him to let him know the food was here, so that's what I set about doing.

Humming "Frosty the Snowman", I sauntered over to his door and knocked with my knuckle. I heard nothing in return, so I pushed it open. The room was empty save for the bathroom door that was cracked.

"I'll just let him know the food is here and tell him I'm gonna wait until he's done," I said out load as I made my way to the door. It was also opened several inches.

When I got to the door, I realized too late the shower faced the opening. Standing there completely naked was Bruno, his hand around the base of his cock, his head tipped back on a groan.

"Holly," he moaned and stroked up to the bulbous tip, swirling the head with his thumb.

Holy fuck! He'd just moaned my name while jacking off. I don't know what in the world prompted me to push open the door and stare as though he was giving me the sexiest private show on earth, but that's exactly what I did.

Bruno was beyond attractive fully clothed. Grumpy, broody, arrogant, but hot as Hades. He knew it. I knew it. Everyone who laid eyes on the man knew it.

Naked, however…utter *perfection*.

His body was a work of art. Beautifully toned arms, thick quads, washboard abs, and squared off pecs. He had a smattering of hair across his chest that made my fingers itch to run them through the tuffs and follow it down to the happy trail leading to the neatly manicured dark curls around his cock. And what a cock it was. Long, thick, maybe slightly above average in size, and hard as a rock. And all of him soaking wet.

"Sweet baby Jesus," I gasped.

Bruno's head turned and his eyes filled with desire as they widened in surprise.

For a full minute, we both stood there staring at one another, his hand on his cock, mine clutching at the door frame.

"The uh, um, ready, food, here," I blundered.

The corner of his mouth tipped up slightly as he turned to face me, his manhood straining up toward his belly button in the most masculine display of his virility. He was sex incarnate, and I wanted a bite so badly.

I mewled at the sight of his stunning manhood, wanting all of that in my mouth, between my thighs, my breasts, whatever, wherever.

"Like what you see?" he rumbled, his voice gritty and raw.

I nodded without thinking, tracing every inch of his slippery chest down, down, down.

He curled his hand around the base of his cock once more and hissed as he stroked along the turgid length.

I licked my lips, watching him pleasure himself as arousal pooled between my own thighs, forcing me to press my legs together wantonly.

"Don't think about it, Holly. Just answer this one question honestly, instinctively. Do you want to join me?"

"Yeah," I breathed, my eyes glued to his hand slowly stroking.

"Holly, take your clothes off. Now." He instructed with a level of authority that made my knees shake. That low tone flowed through me and landed like a pinch to my clit.

I whimpered and did exactly what he instructed, sliding my shorts down my thighs.

"That's a good girl. Now the shirt. Tease me, baby."

I swallowed against the dryness in my throat as I slid my hands up to the first button. He pushed the glass door to the shower stall open and steam billowed out. Sweat prickled against my hairline as he leaned back and pumped his cock in his hand.

With shaking fingers, I released the first button.

My breath hitched as I fingered the second and slowly pushed it through the hole.

"That's it…" he encouraged on a groan, tightening his hold around the glossy tip of his cock. "Now the last button."

I slipped the button through and shrugged my shoulders until the satin fell to the growing puddle at my feet. I was blissfully naked underneath.

"Fucking hell, Holly. You are a goddess. Your body is *unreal.*"

I lifted my hands and cupped my own breasts, pinching the nipples until I cried out, wanting to make him as wild as I felt.

"Get in here," he demanded.

My heart thudded behind my chest, but I pushed my feet to take one step at a time. The second I got close, he pulled me into the shower, turned me around, and pressed me flat to the wall. His slick body plastered against mine as he brought our faces nose to nose. His breath was warm and smelling of whiskey as the steam billowed around us.

"I'm clean. Recently tested. I can have my team send over proof if you need." He got straight to the point.

"I believe you."

"Are you negative and on birth control?" He nuzzled my nose with his own as I ran my hands up and down his slick, muscular back.

"Yeah, and Alana just had us tested. I'm negative too."

"If we do this, we both need to understand exactly what this is." His dark eyes met mine, searching and intense.

"It's just sex." I tilted my head, bringing my mouth closer to his. Our lips just barely touched.

"No strings attached." He cupped the back of my neck and lifted my chin up with his thumb. "Do you understand?"

"I understand," I breathed, rubbing my naked body against his. My breath caught when his cock ground along my clit.

He put his forehead to mine and pumped his hips, rubbing our naked lower bodies together, creating an incredible friction I never wanted to end. Ribbons of electricity flickered along the surface of my skin and spread out through my nerve endings, setting me ablaze.

"This is a bad idea, Holly," he warned.

I wrapped my arms around his neck, brought my mouth to his neck and ran my tongue along it. He tasted of water and a hint of soap. Delicious.

"So what? Fuck me anyway. You need it; I need it."

Within a moment, he had his hands under my ass and my body lifted in the air. I wrapped my legs around his waist, and he was there, *right there*, filling me up. His mouth came down on mine at the exact moment he bottomed out within me.

He silenced my war cry with his mouth, our tongues tangling as he pounded me with his steely length.

I lost myself to the wildness of it all, animal sounds coming from both of us as we fucked one another with abandon. My nails sank into his shoulder blades with each powerful thrust. My cries filled the room as he swirled his hips, finding what he was looking for. And when he did, I screeched as the orgasm flooded my core. I bit down on where his shoulder and neck met while the pleasure ravaged me from top to toe.

He didn't stop.

Before the peak was completely gone, I was pulled off his cock and placed on the bench seat in the corner of the shower. The minute my butt hit the tile, Bruno fell to his knees, the shower battering his back. He didn't say a word when he spread my legs wide open and lifted both of them over his broad shoulders.

"What are you… How are you…" I lost my ability to create a fully formed sentence.

"I need to taste you," he growled and tilted my ass, covering my sex with his mouth.

"Oh my God!" I cried out as his tongue plunged inside, slicking along my over sensitized channel as if he intended to soak up every drop of my release. My head slammed back, and my fingers tunneled into his thick hair as he feasted.

He went down on me as though it was his job, his purpose in life. And when he fluttered that masterful tongue against my clit until I was panting, my thigh muscles quaking, I arched into him, riding the waves of my second climax. He finished by sucking on my clit so hard I saw stars.

I'd never been fucked so hard or so fully in my life.

And he still wasn't done.

After my second orgasm, he lifted my boneless form up into the air, shut off the water and walked us dripping wet into his room. There, he placed me on the bed, flipped me over, and hiked me up onto my hands and knees.

"Hold the position, Holly," he barked, gripping my hips like he owned them. And even with my limbs feeling like nothing but jelly, I did exactly as he ordered, and curled my fingers into the bedding to hold on, because in the span of thirty minutes, I'd become a glutton for anything he wanted to do to me.

He gripped one ass cheek, as he curved his body over mine.

"I'm going to fuck you hard now, Holly. Are you ready, baby?"

"Bruno, please," I begged and wiggled my body with lewd intent.

He chuckled and ran his hand down my spine then palmed both my ass cheeks.

"Your body is a playground," he cooed, his lips kissing the fleshy bits of my butt as he hummed. "So much to play with," he murmured against my skin before spreading my ass cheeks and flicking his tongue against the forbidden hole no man had ever touched.

I gasped and curled inward, and he chuckled.

"I see you're sensitive." He ran his thumb lightly over the puckered flesh teasingly. "Has anyone ever fucked you here?" He dipped his thumb inside just the tiniest bit.

I whimpered at the strange but not unpleasant intrusion, then shook my head.

"Another time perhaps," he said with a sharp smack of my ass.

"Bruno!" I jolted as the skin sizzled at the quick burst of

pain that quickly morphed into simmering, warm heat. I let my forehead fall to the mattress. "Please, please, please," I begged rather incoherently.

"Brace, Holly," was the only warning I got.

Then he was there, up on his knees, one hand curled around my shoulder for leverage, the other on my hip as he plowed inside in a deep thrust.

"Yessssss!" I cried out.

Bruno was a man of his word as he fucked me hard. When I was almost at a third orgasm, he hefted me off my hands and up. "Oh no you don't. You're coming when I say you can come, you hear me?"

"Oh my god, Bruno, Bruno, Bruno," I chanted as he plastered my back to his front, his cock pounding up into me from behind as he used one hand to finger my clit and the other to pluck my nipple.

"I can't hold off, I can't," I shouted, while the walls of my sex clamped down around his brutal thrusts.

"You *can*. You *will*," he commanded.

I could feel his body flex and shudder as he moved. His muscles honed, skin slick with sweat. He made love, or in this case, *fucked*, with every inch of his body. Naturally he found his rhythm, located the hot button within me and stabbed at it repeatedly, manipulating it and me so masterfully I stopped breathing.

"Come, Holly. Come *now*," he whispered in my ear, then nipped at the lobe, sending me spiraling into nirvana.

My body responded instantly, a bomb detonating and taking out an entire block with the force of its blast. I think I blacked out as euphoria flooded my veins and visions of rainbow sparkles speared through my mind.

Behind me, Bruno kept going, until finally, blessedly, he gripped my hips and stilled, his cock unloading his release in wave after beautiful wave.

By the time it was over, I was incapable of moving. So much so, he pulled out, shifted me to my side and kissed my shoulder. "Be right back with a cloth. Don't move."

"Bossy." I mumbled, my eyes already closing as my skin cooled.

In seconds he was back and wiping his release from between my thighs with a warm cloth.

"Mmm, that feels nice," I mumbled.

"Good to know. You rest. I'm going to get our food."

My stomach growled at the mention of food now that we'd sated other baser needs. Not even a minute passed before I could smell the succulent aroma of a five-star restaurant meal. I pushed up onto my side and then crawled over to the head of the bed. Bruno watched as I pulled back the covers and got in and made a "gimmie" gesture with both hands.

He huffed on a smile and shook his head as he approached with my plate. He passed it off to me then turned on the lamp sitting next to the bed. He repeated the process for himself, getting into bed next to me fully naked.

"I thought we were only doing the sex thing, not the couple thing?" I shoved a chunk of savory filet mignon into my mouth then pointed my empty fork at him for emphasis.

He meticulously cut into his steak and turned his head to face me. "We are."

"Then why are we eating dinner together like a date?"

He frowned. "We both gotta eat, and I don't know about you, but I worked up quite the appetite. Besides, how am I supposed to go for another round without sustenance?"

My eyebrows rose straight to my forehead as I held a loaded fork of mashed potatoes over my plate. "Another round?"

That time he grinned wickedly. "I don't know about you, but I was only getting started. It's been weeks since my last hookup."

I licked my lips, tasting the garlic from the potatoes. "It's been longer for me," I admitted.

He shrugged, unbothered as he cut another bite and then looked at me. "Been thinking about your mouth wrapped around my cock all day. I figure we could knock that fantasy out after dinner, then I could eat you for dessert while you have your cake."

My mouth fell open. "Are you always this direct? You know, that could turn a woman off," I sputtered.

What I didn't expect was for him to lean forward, his rainwater scent curling around me as his hand mysteriously snuck under the blanket. I was sitting cross-legged under the covers, my plate teetering on my lap when I felt his hand slide up my inner thigh then cover my sex. He inserted two fingers straight inside as I gripped the edges of my plate and held it aloft, a moan falling on autopilot from my lips.

"I don't know, direct seems to work for some women," he growled, finger-fucking me as he spun his thumb around my clit.

"I, I…uhhhhh, I lost my train of thought," I admitted as he worked me with his hand.

I was just getting into it when he removed his hand. "That's exactly my point," he rumbled on a hiss then sunk those wet fingers into his mouth. He moaned around the two digits before pulling them out, looking me straight in the eye when he said, "You taste like fucking candy. Is that direct enough for you?"

"Mmm hmm," I croaked.

He grinned. "Eat your dinner. Just save room for dessert," he winked.

Turned out, Bruno Castellanos was a man of his word.

After dinner, I sucked his cock until he came down my throat. After, he handed me a new fork and the small plate with a slice of chocolate cake. Then he proceeded to spread my legs and devour *me* while I ate chocolate cake. It was the single most gluttonous, outlandish, and ridiculously hot moment of my life. By the last bite, I was grinding into his face, asking for seconds.

He obliged.

Chapter 9

A Holiday Bang

BRUNO

I woke to a heavy weight sprawled across my chest. My training kicked into high gear as I took a moment to assess the situation, while pretending to be asleep.

The scent of sex, whiskey, and the subtle hint of lavender paired with pine trees filled my nose. Visions of the hours I'd spent fucking Holly last night cascaded through my mind in lavish, fluid technicolor. I lifted my hand and found Holly's lower back, and then her bare bottom. I smiled without even trying as I opened my eyes, allowing them to adjust to the slip of daylight peeking through the space in the curtains. Her glorious hair was fanned across my chest and fell like golden waterfalls over the sides of my ribs. Little puffs of air spilled from her lips as she exhaled, still asleep.

She was so damn beautiful. Strikingly so.

But none of that shocked me. What was blowing my mind, and making my toes curl and my balls ache, was what was happening down under.

I was hard.

Painfully so.

And I was still *inside* her.

The insatiable fucking got so out of hand last night, we both fell asleep with my dick still in her.

I grinned at the insanity of that thought. It sure as hell had never happened to me before. I couldn't even remember the last time I'd slept next to a woman the entire night let alone fallen completely asleep while still connected physically. Usually, sex was a pleasurable transaction with a woman I met while in a strange city on a job. A hookup for lack of a better term.

Holly, on the other hand, was no hookup. Technically, she was a client, or more accurately, contracted to a client. Did that make it better or worse? Fuck if I knew. The only thing I did know, right in that moment, was that she was the best sex of my life. And I've had a lot of sex. In my line of business, personal connection and physical touch don't often come together. With Holly, everything was different. Better.

My carnal, nearly animalistic side came out in full force last night. Moreover, so did hers. That woman was no prey. She participated in the hunt for pleasure just as avidly as I did. The two of us feeding off one another. And to hell with stopping that train once it left the station. I was ravenous in my pursuit of every moan, groan, and cry for God. By the end of the night, I wasn't sure if I was God, Bruno, or just Oh. All I knew was that I couldn't stop. Didn't want to, either. Every time I looked into her eyes, kissed her lips, tasted that sweet nectar between her thighs, or so much as spied a new freckle I hadn't noticed previously, my dick went hard.

It was absolutely unheard-of behavior for me. Picture snaps of different things we experienced last night claimed my mind like a sexy movie reel.

Holly laughed. My dick went hard.

Holly sighed. My dick went hard.

Holly begged for more. My dick went hard.

Holly *breathed*…my dick went hard.

Before I knew what was happening, my hips were pistoning up as I pressed Holly's ass down, piercing her as deeply as possible in one go. She woke on a throaty moan, her body working along with mine as I fucked her fully awake. She curved her spine forward, squeezed her thighs, and clamped those wicked tight muscles around my length in a vise grip, unlike any other.

With both of her hands pressed on each side of my body she pushed her upper half up, and arched her body back, her tits bouncing into place, nipples erect and pointed to the sky.

"God what a wake-up call," she breathed, her hands leisurely flowing into her hair and holding it up messily as she rode my cock with greater purpose. I gripped her hips and pumped up every time she came down.

"Fuck yes!" she swore, picking up her pace, her tits bouncing enticingly.

"Get there, Holly," I gritted through clenched teeth, then glided a thumb over her wet bundle of nerves and spun circles around it.

I watched with lurid fascination as my cock split and stretched those pretty pink lower lips wide, our combined arousal from last night and today coating her path in a vulgar graphic display that I'd be fantasizing about for months, if not years. The slippery wet, squelching sounds our bodies made with each upward drive had me out of my mind with lust.

"You. Are. So. Damn. Hot. I never want to stop fucking you!" I roared, using my abdominal muscles to spear up as she bore down. The moment her soft blonde curls crashed to meet my dark ones, her body clamped around the base of my cock, and I lost it.

Together we fell over the ledge straight into an ocean of endless pleasure.

For at least ten minutes, we lay there silently, her once again sprawled across my chest, both content to live within our own thoughts as we came down from the high. Once I felt I had my libido in check, I cupped her bottom, giving her a little jiggle.

"You dead?" I asked.

"Yep," she popped out a puff of air as she enunciated the 'p' in the word.

I glanced over at the wall clock across from the bed. "You have to be in the beauty chair by ten a.m."

"Mmm hmm. Thanks for the reminder." She yawned and then hissed as my cock finally went soft and slipped from her body. "Five more minutes," she sighed and snuggled my chest like a baby kitten. I wrapped my arms around her, holding her close.

Damn, I could get used to this.

The thought lasted a whole two seconds before the titanium emotional wall I had built between me and my feelings slammed down, breaking the connection, and I let my arms drop to my sides.

"You sure? It's 9:25 now…"

That caught her attention.

Within half a breath she'd jumped up and out of bed. I barely registered her naked ass swaying before it disappeared through the door, likely headed to her own room. The sound of a shower starting sealed the deal.

It didn't take me long to get ready for the day. I showered, dressed in my preferred all-black suit and black accessories, including my double gun shoulder harness, and was ready to go within fifteen minutes. My hair was still wet as I made coffee. I could hear Holly running around her room talking to herself.

"How do you like your coffee?" I called out.

"Black is fine!" she responded.

Me too.

By the time the coffee was brewed and poured into the to-go paper cups with lids the hotel so helpfully supplied, she was exiting her room. She wore a men's button-up, white sleeveless shirt, with a black bra that showed entirely through the thin fabric, not to mention the front only had one button fastened. I didn't like seeing another man's shirt flirt along her bare skin so casually, as if it was a perfectly normal day for her.

Did it once belong to an ex-boyfriend?

I made a mental note to find out her dating history. Maybe Jonas could pull some additional information.

Stand down, Bruno, I suddenly reminded myself.

This was not my woman. She could wear what she wanted. Besides, doing a deeper dive than what the client wants, expects, and has paid for, is a blatant misuse of our talents, not to mention treading a little too close to ethical boundaries. I didn't *need* to know who she'd been with romantically in order to guard her body or fuck her into next week.

The frustrating thing was I *wanted* to know.

Desperately.

I coughed and attempted to clear my throat at the sight of all that succulent Holly flesh. Under the dress shirt she wore a body-hugging miniskirt showing off her mile-long legs. On her feet, she wore thin, black, flip-flops.

I pushed the personal thoughts away and focused on the problem in front of me, including our lack of time to talk over what happened between us and how we were going to move forward.

"We've got five minutes to get you up to Alana's office for your beauty appointment and subsequent date with Mr. Hollywood."

Her eyes lit up at the mention of the actor she was to

accompany tonight. Part of me loathed and loved that fact. Loathed because I didn't want her being excited to date someone else, and loved because the sooner we had some separation from one another, the better. Which made me think about handing over her protection to another one of my men. As soon as that idea hit, I dismissed it entirely. There wasn't anyone else besides Jonas that I'd trust to protect her. Which created a whole new problem. I fucking liked the woman. More than I should.

"I'm ready when you are." She sipped her coffee and hummed.

That hum reminded me of when her lips were wrapped tightly around my cock, and I was fucking her throat. *She took me so deep...*

"Fuck me," I grumbled underneath my breath and rubbed at my temples with thumb and forefinger.

"What was that?" she asked, pulling her purse up over her shoulder as I abruptly turned around and headed toward the door.

"Nothing. Let's go."

She flip-flopped after me, her shoes smacking noisily on the tile. "Should we, uh, maybe talk about last night? I don't think Alana would be upset if we were maybe ten minutes late."

I stooped at the door. "There's really nothing to say..."

Her head jerked back. "Really? Nothing? I think a dozen orgasms between us warrants at least a little bit of conversation, wouldn't you agree?" She smiled playfully then nudged my shoulder.

I inhaled fully and let it out slowly, feeling much like an irritated dragon that would much rather use fire to burn the entire world down than have this conversation.

"We had sex." Unbelievable sex, but I left that part out, trying not to encourage her. This type of conversation was often difficult at best, and in my experience, letting someone down the day after sex could also be brutal. Always best to cut the cord before anyone got hurt, is what Jonas recommended.

"We had a lot of sex, Bruno. A lot, a lot, a lot of sex, buddy," she crossed her arms over one another and waited for me to speak.

She could wait all day. Whoever starts the argument loses. Period.

"I just want to make sure we're cool. It was good. But that's all it was," she shared, her voice becoming gentle.

"Good?"

She grinned, her entire face lighting up as her cheeks bloomed a rosy hue. "Okay, phenomenal. I haven't been bedded like that in…well, ever. You are seriously amazing, Bruno. Who knew you had it in you?" She patted my chest in a placating manner I didn't quite understand.

I frowned, not having any idea where this conversation was now going. I'd expected her to be clingy and needy today, but what I was getting wasn't that. Not even in the same hemisphere.

"What are you trying to say, Holly?"

"You know…well…" She licked her lips and bit into the bottom one, her gaze jumping from place to place. Everywhere but my eyes. "You're about to be on a date with me and another guy. Are you going to be okay with that?"

I snorted. "Am I going to be okay? Are you being serious right now?"

Her eyes bugged out to the size of dinner plates. "Um, yeah. I just want to make sure to reiterate what we agreed on last night. No strings attached. Just sex. Because I'm in this for real. I need to get chosen. What I don't need is another man getting in the way of what I'm trying to do to start my future."

I burst out laughing. "Un-fucking-believable. You are one of a kind, lady. Usually, I'm the one that has to have this conversation with the women I fuck, and here you are…what?

Letting me down easy." I shook my head. "For fuck's sake. Let's go." I waved her to follow. "You're going to be late." And on that note, I turned around and left our hotel room, her shoes flip-flapping along as she brought up the rear. We passed my men on the way to the elevator. I made sure to give them each eye contact and a nod of my head in greeting and respect.

That did not, however, take away from my thoughts about what Holly said back in our room.

The nerve. Letting me down easy. Please. Now I had a point to prove.

The only thing that would be going down was her, to her fucking knees in an airplane bathroom. Maybe while her pretty boy actor was pouring champagne, waiting for her, she'd be swallowing my cock like she did so perfectly last night.

An evil smile adorned my lips as I stared at my reflection in the elevator's mirrored doors.

"What has you smiling like that?"

"How are you on airplanes?"

Chapter 10

Your Sleigh Awaits

HOLLY

Today was the day I would change my entire life. And what a day it would be. Jet-setting across the West Coast in a glamourous designer gown and shoes. Attending a real Hollywood elite event while on the arm of a famous movie star. I could hardly believe this was my life. At least for today it was.

Alana had informed my suitor or in this case, my bidder, that he could meet us in the lobby bar of the hotel where she worked and lived part of the year. The rest of the time Alana resided in France with her husband Cristophe, whom I'd come to adore. He was the golden retriever to Alana's black cat personality. A perfect match.

After the glam team did the full gambit of hair, makeup and attire this morning, I felt prepared for whatever the day would bring. Truly, I'd never looked better or felt more beautiful.

Bruno, however, snarled at the sight of my complete look, preferring to glare at me and everyone in the room before ditching us for a phone call with a member of his team. His response had hurt my feelings a little. We'd had such an incredible night together, one I wouldn't soon to forget. I assumed we'd have a deeper connection today. A friendship of sorts. I mean, we'd spent most of the previous evening naked and fucking each other's brains out. That should have earned me a "you look great," or "that color suits you."

Something.

But no. I got Mr. Grumpy Pants back in full force. Even now, as we waited at the bar and I sipped a glass of champagne, he was in full brood, choosing to sit several seats away from Alana and myself. He claimed it was to give us some privacy.

"Holly, I presume?" A man spoke as he tapped me on the shoulder.

Alana rose from her seat as I spun my chair around. Instantly, I was struck dumb, meeting Mr. Hollywood, I mean, Colin Omstead in person. He was unbelievably good looking, almost painfully so. Reminded me of attempting to look at the sun to watch a solar eclipse. Beautiful but dangerous to one's health.

Colin was tall, with wide shoulders that tapered into the classic V-shape at his waist. Perfect dirty blonde hair and startling clear blue eyes. His eyes had the subtlest crinkle at the edges, showing his thirty-five years of life on this Earth, but they didn't distract from his beauty in the slightest. In fact, they added to it. He wore a crisp, classic black tuxedo, with a daring dark-green satin tie and pocket square that matched my dress exactly. He looked dashing, like a real-life Prince Charming. And then he *smiled*, showing a set of pearly white teeth, prettier than my dentist had, and I swooned.

My head felt light, my feet heavy, and my knees wobbly.

"And you're Colin," I breathed, pure awe stealing my

ability to speak normally.

He extended his hand and I quickly wiped mine on my cocktail napkin before I shook his. Electricity sparked at the center of our palms, sending a wave of gooseflesh across my bare arms.

"Guilty," he purred, and leaned closer to kiss my cheek.

My heart pounded against my chest as I inhaled his cologne. It was divine—cedar and citrus.

Colin pulled away and repeated the process with Alana, only he did not kiss her cheek.

"Mr. Omstead, this is my belle of the ball. I expect you will take great care of her. When shall I expect her return?"

Did Alana just pull the mom card? I wasn't a teenager. I'd been a full-grown adult for over a decade. At thirty-years-old, I didn't need another maternal figure attempting to manage my time. One mother was plenty.

"Oh, Alana, I'm a very big girl. I think I've got this covered…"

Alana smiled in that serene way that put everyone at ease. "You misunderstand, *chérie*. It is my responsibility to ensure the safety and comfort of both my candidates and…" she glanced around the bar, likely assessing how close other patrons were to us. "Clients." She chose the word wisely, preferring not to use the term bidder in mixed company it seemed.

"Not to worry, Madam Toussaint," Bruno interrupted. "I'll be chaperoning them the entire evening."

"Excuse me?" Colin frowned. "I assure you, I have nothing but honorable intentions with Ms. Knight. And my security team will be with us to and from the event, as well as escorting us to the hotel."

"Hotel?" I cut in. "I didn't pack a bag. I assumed we'd be returning to Las Vegas."

"These things often run very late. I took the liberty of securing us suites in the host hotel and securing any essentials you might need, including clothing for tomorrow. All of your sizes were on your candidate card. My pilot wasn't able to get clearance to fly back to Las Vegas this evening, so I made appropriate arrangements. We will return after breakfast tomorrow morning."

"Sounds like you've worked it all out. Are we ready to go?" I asked.

"Not so fast." Bruno lifted a hand. "I'm Bruno Castellanos, Ms. Knight's personal security. I will be attending and keeping Holly"—Alana glared at the casual familiarity—"I mean *Ms. Knight*, within my eyesight throughout the evening as outlined in great detail within the contract. Candidate security is of utmost importance."

"I-I see." Colin reluctantly agreed.

My eyes widened and my temperature shot through the roof as anger spiraled through my bloodstream. I held up a finger. "Just a moment," I snapped.

With little thought to who was watching, I pushed through our little huddle, my hands planted directly on Bruno's chest as I maneuvered him a solid ten feet down the bar.

"I don't need a babysitter!" I hissed.

"Don't you?" he murmured, his gaze on Alana and Colin behind me.

I speared at his chest roughly. "No, I don't! And you better behave, or I swear to God I'll…"

He wrapped his hand around mine at his chest, bent his body forward and put his lips next to my ear. A shiver raced down my spine at the contact, and I gasped.

"You'll what?" He hummed and my core tightened at that low rumble. "You sure as hell liked it when I called you *baby* last night, when I was balls deep inside of you."

Arousal and fury pulsated through my body, especially between my legs. Still, I needed to persevere. He was being an absolute dick. *"Bruno,"* I warned, letting my tone fill in the blanks. "You will not ruin this for me. You said sex only, no strings. This feels like a whole lot of strings!"

"Maybe I changed my mind," he sneered.

That had me jolting away, shaking my head. "No." I growled. "You don't get to do that. This is my life, and my choice. And I choose to go on this date. Now you better get it together, real freakin' quick." I huffed, plastered a smile on my face, and turned around.

"I think we're all in agreement. I'm ready when you are, Colin," I announced, sauntering over to my date. I was proud of myself for not breaking down, or reading too much into Bruno's loose suggestion that there might be more between us. He was the one that set the parameters in the first place. I was simply following them. Sex was sex. Sure, it was beyond good, a night I'll never forget in my wildest dreams, but that didn't give him the right to mess this up for me.

He promised.

Did he promise, though?

I shook my head and looped my arm with Colin's. "I'm excited about tonight and getting to know you better."

He put his hand over mine and gave me another megawatt smile. "Your sleigh awaits."

The jet was luxe. A level of opulence I wasn't accustomed to. The last time I was on a plane was with a few friends, when we spent a week in Cancun, partying it up. Those seats were coach, at the very back of the plane, and I'd been sandwiched between a mother holding a crying baby and a big guy that was so tall his knees touched the seat in front of him, and his head towered over the seats. He also fell asleep with his head on my shoulder and drooled on my ruffly blouse. This was not that.

"Wow," I whispered in awe as Colin pointed to a full-sized, leather lounge chair. I slid into the seat as gracefully as possible in a beaded, figure-hugging gown.

Bruno glided past, winking at me as he did so. I wanted to punch him in the face and kiss him in equal measure. He was muddling my mind. When he claimed to have changed his mind about us, I had no idea what that meant. Moreover, I believed any change wasn't due to him actually having real feelings for me, but because another man was in the picture. In my experience, men could be like dogs. Inappropriately marking territory that wasn't theirs.

I forced myself not to respond and, instead, patted the seat next to me for Colin.

He sat down and ordered champagne for the two of us from the flight attendant. Once we received our drinks, the captain announced we were ready for takeoff.

I hated this part of flying, so I closed my eyes, gripped the armrest and started my prayers. I always repeated the "Our Father" until the plane leveled out and reached its cruising altitude. Only this time, I didn't expect to have a warm hand cover mine. I opened my eyes and stared into the pretty blue skies that were in Colin's eyes, reflecting the clouds from the open airplane window opposite him.

"Hey there," he said and interlaced our fingers. "We're almost to the easy part," he encouraged.

I smiled and leaned my head against the back of the seat and lost myself in his gaze.

"You're kind." I murmured.

"And you're stunning," he whispered back.

"Thank you for choosing me to go on this date with you."

"Thank you for agreeing to it. I have to admit, when Alana

sent your photo over, I just knew I had to meet you."

I squeezed his hand. "I'll admit to being rather shell-shocked when she told me who my first date would be. I mean…you could have anyone," I shook my head. "Why do you even need the auction?"

He let go of my hand and the air between us cooled.

"I'm sorry; that was rude. It's your business and none of mine."

He sighed and ran his hand through his hair. "No, it's a fair question. And something we'll need to work out later if we…"

"Get married?"

He exhaled sharply and chuckled. "Are you always this direct?"

A rough laugh came from somewhere behind us.

Holy shit. Colin had just asked the exact same question to me that I'd asked of Bruno last night. I wanted to jump up and demand Bruno shut his sexy face and leave us alone, but that would only egg him on.

"When it's important, yeah, I am."

"My job, my life's work is amazing, and I've been very lucky to earn the roles I've played. But with great rewards come great sacrifices. Usually in the privacy department. My life isn't always my own. Carving out private time is crucial and somewhat few and far between. My fans are great. The best really. It's just I'm always under a microscope and whoever I date will be too."

Jesus. I hadn't considered what my role in this relationship would be other than wife to a famous guy. It never dawned on me that I would also become a source of media interest.

"I see you're putting the ugly pieces together. Already, the paparazzi are going to go crazy when they see you on my arm tonight. Anyone I bring to anything will receive such interest. Did Alana prepare you for that?"

I shook my head and then nodded, not wanting to throw

Alana under the bus. She was the woman handing me everything I could ever want, plus it was her limo that rode in to save me during my darkest hour. Bruno may have been the muscle, but she was the catalyst, and I'd be forever grateful.

"I'm not scared." *I was terrified,* but my mother always told me to 'fake it until you make it' and that is exactly what I planned to do in this circumstance.

"Does anything scare you?" He lifted his hand and ran a single finger along my jawline. When he got to my ear, he traced the column of my neck to the strap of my gown.

I swallowed against the sudden thrill of his featherlight touch teasing along my skin.

"Um…spiders?"

He burst out laughing, the sexual tension in the air cooling. He leaned back and took my hand once more and picked up his champagne flute.

"A toast," he gestured to my glass.

I lifted mine between us.

"To the beginning of our story."

"I like that," I agreed and clinked my glass lightly with his.

"Me too. Now, tell me about yourself. I want to know everything." He beamed.

I got comfortable, settling back in the butter-soft leather chair and told him about my life. How I grew up in Las Vegas, that my parents were an avid and active part of my life, and that I'd stop at nothing to see my dreams come true.

"And is that why you joined the auction? To open your own bar one day?"

"Yeah. I love being around people all the time, serving them drinks, learning their journeys. However, at my establishment we'll have the coolest décor, interesting mixed drinks, live music regularly, open mic nights for the comedians and more. I want to set up a place where the regular citizens of Las Vegas could go to be part of their community."

"So not a tourist trap?"

"Nope. I even toyed with the idea that, in order to get in, you needed to have a Las Vegas ID, but that could limit sales too much and cause problems. My ultimate goal is to have a place where the people who live here feel it is their own. And I want to hire both my parents and give them a super loaded retirement. They've devoted their entire lives to me and one another. To this day, they both work in the same casino. He's a dealer, she's a waitress. I want them to work with me on something that can be family owned. A place for us to be together without any worries."

"And what if your bar becomes too popular and there ends up being a line around the block?" he asked in a tone that made the hairs on the back of my neck tingle. Like he knew something I didn't.

"I don't know. The thought never entered my mind. I can't imagine something I owned being that outrageous. Being super rich wasn't exactly part of my plan. Having a place that was my own and could also provide for my aging parents, setting us all up for a comfortable life a bit better than we have now is the goal."

His jaw firmed and a muscle in his cheek ticked.

"Why do I feel like you're upset all of a sudden?"

He shook his head abruptly. "It's nothing. Don't worry about it." He patted my knee in a placating manner that sent red warning flags waving in the back of my mind.

I turned to face him. "I'm not the kind of girl to let something go so quickly. I'm also not cool with allowing uncomfortable feelings to stew. I'd like you to share your thoughts with me. Honesty between couples is important. No, it's *everything*."

He closed his eyes and sighed. "It's just that, if this thing with us continues, and already I'm liking the visual of us being together…" he added with such an earnest expression, my heart clenched.

"I like that visual too," I admitted. I could absolutely see myself with this hunky sweet guy, more so than the uptight, grumpy, alpha a-hole that fucked like a God.

"If you opened up an establishment, in Las Vegas, hell *anywhere*, and you were married to me, it would get a lot of press."

"That would be a good thing though, wouldn't it?" I tried to lighten the vibe he was putting off.

He shook his head. "You don't understand. If you were with me, and the press or fans found out about your bar, you would be mobbed every night."

I frowned. "Oh…that could pose some problems."

"Yeah. It definitely would mean your vision would have to change. You wouldn't be able to work the bar in person. I wouldn't recommend your parents doing so either. The media and fans can be rabid for information about me and whoever I date. You could own a bar. Many in fact. But my wife and her family actually working in public jobs…" He shook his head. "Not possible."

My stomach dropped, making me feel nauseous.

"But truly, it would be okay," he squeezed my hand. "Because you wouldn't need the money if you were married to me. I'd take care of everything. You, your parents. All would be well."

All would be well.

All would be well.

All would NOT be well.

My heart thundered in my chest; sweat beaded at my hairline and under my arms. My hands shook as I placed the champagne glass down and stood abruptly. My knees wanted to give out, but I held my balance.

"I've… Uh, I've got to use the ladies room," I croaked.

I dashed to the back of the plane and fumbled around the three doors until I felt a presence at my back.

"Breathe, Holly," Bruno whispered in my ear as his arm

came around my waist, pressing my back against him, soothing my fear instantly.

I trembled in his arms as he opened a door, pushed me inside, and followed me in.

"I'm going to lose it," I clipped, tears filling my eyes as my body and mind freaked the fuck out by what Colin had just shared.

"You're okay," he whispered. "You're okay. Breathe, baby." He held me close as I gasped in air like a deep-sea diver just reaching the surface of the water. "I'm here. You're okay. Breathe in with me," he commanded and inhaled. I synced my breathing with his, sucking in air rabidly. "Slow it down." He put one of his hands over my heart. "Fuck," he hissed. "Your heartbeat is too fast. Keep breathing with me," he encouraged, and I nodded, matching his breaths, my gaze focused entirely on his in our reflection in the mirror.

When I was breathing more normally, he placed a warm line of kisses from my shoulder to my ear. "What happened?" he flicked his tongue in the space he knew from last night was an erogenous zone for me.

I moaned and closed my eyes. "Nothing, I...I just..."

The hand that was over my heart, shifted, his fingers tracing the lace cup of my dress. "Tell me..." he said, sliding his hand inside my dress, cupping my breasts just the way I liked, with firm pressure.

The distraction was exactly what I needed. I gasped at the glorious pleasure, the exact opposite of the chaotic fear that had rampaged through me only minutes ago.

"I-I freaked out," I admitted.

"Mmmhmm." His hips pressed me against the bathroom vanity, his thumb and forefinger plucking at my nipple making it hard. I arched back, rubbing my ass against his hardened cock, losing myself to the bliss of his touch.

"Why did you freak out?" His teeth skimmed along my

shoulder while his other hand slipped around my front thigh, finding the slit in the green glimmering fabric.

"*Bruno*," I breathed his name, not knowing whether to tell him to stop or to continue. All I knew was I had gone from scared out of my mind, to wanting nothing but his hands on me.

"I'm right here," he growled, that sneaky hand slipping beneath the fabric of my dress to find my lace panties. It was nothing for him to work his hand inside them and then he was… "Right there," he groaned and plunged two fingers inside me. I lifted up onto my toes as he went deeper, his thumb coming up to work my clit masterfully.

"Oh my God," I sighed on a moan.

"There you go again, calling me God." He laughed low and gruff as he fingered me.

"What are you doing to me?" I asked, shamelessly working my hips, chasing the pleasure I knew he could give.

"I'm bringing you back to reality." He pushed his fingers deeper, found the spot I needed, and doubling his efforts, massaged it relentlessly.

Sparks flew between us as my entire body gave in to his every whim. Heat flooded my core as my nerve endings went berserk. I whimpered and flowed with his movements, my hips thrusting desperately.

"I'm going to come," I mewled.

"I know, baby. Come all over my fingers and then later, after your date with another man, I'll fuck you so good you won't even remember the movie star's name." He pinched my clit, and I soared, anger and passion mixing like a lethal poison as I clamped my hand over my own mouth and came hard.

He rode the wind with me until I finally came down, but when I did come down, I met his gaze in the mirror.

His smug expression undid all the pleasure I'd just experienced.

"I fucking hate you."

Chapter 11

Nutcrackers and Nonsense

BRUNO

"I fucking hate you." Holly sneered after I'd given her what I thought was one banger of an orgasm.

The second I removed my hand from between her soaked thighs and the other from her diamond-hard nipple, she twirled around and smacked me in the face, then screeched like a hyena, grabbed me by the lapels, and crashed her lips over mine.

I drank from the well of her mouth, our tongues tangling as one hand went into her hair, the other to her ass. I ground against her as my cheek sizzled with heat from where she'd clocked me. She groaned angrily and bit down on my bottom lip so hard she may have drawn blood, before ripping her mouth away and shoving me backward.

"Mixed messages much?" I scowled, rubbing my jaw, then my lip to find a drop of blood where she'd bitten me.

"How dare you!" she hissed under her breath.

"How dare me? You're the one that smacked me and then kissed me," I griped.

"Because you played me like a fiddle with your sexy, broody, voodoo that you have over me. I am on a date and you just…you just…"

"Fingered you until you came hard and helped you down from a massive panic attack? Yes, yes, I did."

She frowned. "That was a panic attack?"

"Yeah. Something Mr. Hollywood said set you off. I came to help. And I did. Don't you feel better?" I smirked, bringing the two fingers I had inside of her moments ago to my mouth and sucking on them. I groaned when her sweet flavor lit up my tastebuds, making me want to lift her ass onto the vanity and eat direct from the source right now.

Her eyes first sparked with what I knew to be lust, but quickly morphed into anger. "Don't do that again. I'm on a date with another man."

"I won't if you won't." I smirked, as her eyes narrowed to slits.

A knock on the door broke us from our bitch fest staring contest.

"Holly, you okay in there?" Colin spoke through the door.

"Speaking of the devil…" I put my hand to the doorknob as Holly scrambled to stop me by batting at my hands.

"No!" she hissed but it was too late.

I opened the door and grinned at the concerned, then surprised face of the man I currently loathed.

"Holly wasn't feeling well." I patted my chest pocket nonchalantly as though I had something inside, which I did not. "I gave her some anti-nausea pills. She should be okay by the time we arrive, but she should rest. Right, Holly?" I turned to face her.

She ran her hands down her body, righting herself, but had no idea how it looked more like a sensual caress along her gorgeous frame. I noticed it, and so did Mr. Hollywood, as could be seen by the way his gaze traced her curves as though he was imagining her sans the dress. I gritted my teeth and did my best not to reach for my holster.

"I've got it, Mr. Castellanos," Colin murmured, reaching a helping hand out for Holly.

"Of course. I'll be in my seat if you need me again, Holly."

Her head lifted, and her fiery gaze met mine. While Colin was doting on her, I brought the two fingers that I'd just had inside her sweet heat up to my face and brazenly inhaled. "Mmm, I sure am hungry."

Holly's mouth dropped open, and her gaze went lazy, the same way it did when I was about to feast on her.

"Yeah, I can't wait to eat. *I'm starved.* Maybe a steak or... chocolate cake. What do you say, Holly? I know chocolate cake is your favorite." I tilted my head and watched her squirm, likely remembering how much I ravaged her while she gorged on cake last night.

"I don't think we have any on the plane right now, but maybe some cookies," Colin suggested.

"No bother, I'll save my appetite for later." I pursed my lips and blew Holly a kiss when Colin was facing the other way.

She shook her head and glared.

Oh, tonight was going to be such fun. I now knew exactly how to get under Holly's skin and in her panties.

Colin Omstead didn't have a chance in hell of winning this woman. I just needed to figure out what that meant for the auction and for *me,* because I didn't want to let her go, but I also had no idea how to offer her more.

The red-carpet scene was a nightmare right out of a horror themed Christmas movie. Not only was the entire hotel draped in decorative Christmas lights, complete with twenty-foot-tall wooden Nutcrackers framing its entrance, there were paparazzi with flashing cameras and screaming fans everywhere. Only in LA would you find giant Nutcrackers and fake snow when the temperature outside was a cool seventy-five degrees. None of it made any sense and was entirely overdone.

When Colin alighted from the limo and held a hand out for Holly, the crowd surrounding the event went wild. The pitch and volume of the roar practically made my ears bleed.

Instantly, I went for Holly's arm, but Colin stepped in front of me. "I've got it from here," he barked, staking his claim the same way I would have if our situations were reversed.

I nodded and stood back, creating a barrier between the couple and the crowd. Colin's security team had the other side and the back of the huddle we'd created. We were stationed right outside of the hotel in front of a set of stairs leading to the entrance. The red carpet ran from the curb all the way up and over the stairs into the building. Red ropes were strung on each side of the walkway separating the crowd and paparazzi from the celebrities arriving. I had no idea this event would be this massive. Colin's security team did not provide the appropriate intel.

My internal safety meter was starting to buzz, sending red flags waving in every direction. I clocked the number of guards stationed on both sides and quickly realized there was a distinct lack of security based on the amount of people clamoring to gain access to the stars.

I wanted to get Holly inside right fucking now.

What I didn't expect when I turned around to suggest we get moving, was for Colin to put his arm around Holly's waist, holding her far more intimately than warranted. It suggested to the crowd that they were on more than just a date. He doubled down when he planted them both in the center of the carpet allowing everyone and their brother to take pictures of them. The photographers went nuts screaming at the duo.

"Colin, Colin, who's with you tonight?"

"Who's the blonde bombshell?"

"Is that your girlfriend?"

Colin didn't say a word. He just stood there and let them assume she was more than just a date while they took endless photos. He could have so easily claimed Holly was a friend, to keep her safest, but no, he wanted them to see her as a romantic interest. Which ultimately would play into his story when he bought her hand in the auction, and they got married so suddenly.

That motherfucker.

And what about Holly?

What I overheard before Holly had her panic attack was that he'd insinuated he would take care of her and her family. I could fucking take care of her and her family just as well as Mr. Hollywood, but that wasn't what Holly wanted. She had goals and dreams for herself. Things she wanted to accomplish on her own, not by being hand-fed buckets of money in exchange for the price of her dreams.

Finally, the next car rolled up and the attendants urged them to follow the carpet up the stairs, past all the fans, to enter the hotel where the event was being held.

I followed at Holly's side, a few feet away, matching what Colin's security did, giving them space but also staying close. My gaze cataloged everyone near them to ascertain any potential threats. What I didn't expect was a woman holding a microphone to duck under the red ropes, race over like an Olympian track runner and clock Holly in the head with the microphone, then bodily fling herself at Colin. He caught the woman, but that didn't stop the fifty other screaming fans from doing the same and bum rushing our group.

Holly screamed at the top of her lungs, a sound that pierced my heart like a dart hitting a bullseye. I watched in dread as her body bowed forward and she reached for her forehead. I went to counter the action, immediately bodily pushing people away from her until I finally scooped Holly up, spun us around, and raced up the steps that led inside.

The crowd mobbed Colin so completely his blonde head disappeared in the crowd as the security around them flung people off him trying to reach their charge. His own security had jumped over him, the way a pair of defenders on an NFL league would protect their quarterback.

Me, I protected the real prize…Holly.

When I got her inside, her entire body was shaking, her hands covering her forehead. "Baby, are you okay? Let me see your head," I begged, cupping her cheeks.

Her face was ghost white; her expression frightened, those pretty eyes of her shifting aimlessly as though she was lost.

"I've got you. You hear me?"

She nodded and let me gently remove her hand from her forehead. There was already a massive bump appearing, swollen pink tissue bulging where the woman hit her. Holly didn't take her eyes off me, her hands clutching my forearms as I assessed the wound.

"Excuse me, miss." A hotel attendant approached and touched her elbow. She flinched, let out a little cry, and plowed into my chest, tucking her face against me as the tears came.

"Back the fuck off!" I bellowed and wrapped my arms around her while she sobbed. "Lead us to the doctor. I know you have one at fancy events like this."

He nodded, clearly rattled as he waved me over toward an empty hall.

I picked up Holly as she continued to cry against my chest and rushed down the hall to an open hotel room. Inside was a man in a suit, a stethoscope dangling around his neck.

"Oh, my goodness, please, place her here," he encouraged, gesturing to the sofa.

Holly clung to me when I tried to set her down, so I sat with her in my lap.

"What happened?" The doctor asked, genuinely concerned. "Heat? Too much alcohol?"

"She was hit on the head by a psycho fan of Colin Omstead's," I grated, the situation becoming all too clear now that my girl was being tended to.

"Oh dear. May I?" He waved his hand toward Holly.

"Holly, baby, the doctor needs to see your head." I ran my fingers along the side of her hair, pushing the long golden locks over her shoulder.

She sniffled and then sat up a little straighter while still in my lap. Her head turned and the doctor grimaced.

"Looks like you got clobbered good. I'm just going to shine this light into your eyes, and ask that you follow it for me," he turned a pen light on and moved it around. "Looks good. I'm going to inspect the injury, okay?"

I liked this doctor's approach. He asked for permission and told her exactly what he was going to do.

The doc reached out and used his thumbs to manipulate the wound, feeling around it. "Can you get me an icepack from the little fridge over there?" he requested of the attendant who'd followed us in and hadn't left.

The attendant did as the doctor bade.

"We're going to have you sit here with the ice on your forehead for a little while, see if we can't get some of that swelling down. Do you know if you lost consciousness at all? Even for a second?"

Holly shook her head. "I didn't black out; it just hurts a lot."

"I'll bet. Was anyone else with you?" he asked, and as if the devil himself had risen straight from hell, I could hear a man screaming Holly's name.

Eventually, a slew of people, Colin leading the pack, raced into the room. His tie was half off, his shirt ripped and his hair a bird's nest on his head. There were lipstick stains all over his face, hands, and neck.

"Holly! My God, are you okay?" He stormed forward and fell to his knees before us, attempting to reach out to touch what was not his.

"You can back up, Mr. Omstead," I clung to my precious cargo. "Give her some space," I demanded in a tone that would be followed or consequences would ensue.

"Colin," Holly whispered dejectedly before her face crumpled into despair and the tears made a second appearance.

"She's clearly upset after being attacked." For the second time in just over a week, I wanted to say, but wasn't about to share Holly's personal life with this do-gooder loser.

"I can't believe that happened. The event swore there was security up and down the carpet. If I had known it would be so easy for the fans to break through the barricade, we would have gone through the rear private entrance. I'm so so sorry," he reached out as if to console her.

I boldly shoved his hand away. "No *fucking* touching."

Holly reached for my hand and patted it, before clearing her throat and sliding off my lap and to my side. "Thank you, Bruno." Her eyes met mine. "Thank you for saving me… again."

"Again?" Colin asked, confused.

"Shut it!" I barked at him.

"Hey?" Holly cupped my cheek. "Look at me."

I glared at Colin and then turned my head, her eyes were filled with gratitude and something I didn't want to name but it looked a lot like trust.

"Thank you for saving me, Bruno. That could have been really bad without you there."

"It's my job," I said on autopilot. "It was my honor," I corrected, letting down that mental wall between me and my feelings for just a moment. The experience was unusual and made me itch to get up and do something, anything, but instead, I forced myself to take it in, to look into Holly's warm gaze and accept her thanks. "You're welcome."

She nodded and then shifted to face Colin. "Are you okay?"

I gritted my teeth and let her do her thing.

"Fine. I mean, that was scary. It hasn't been that bad in years, but I'm more worried about you." His gaze went to her forehead where the ugly bump was getting uglier by the second.

"Ice," I reminded her.

She placed the icepack back over the injury and winced. "I'll try to rally, maybe the doctor can give me some pain meds so I could stay…"

"Absolutely not!" I said at the same time Colin did.

At least we agreed on something.

"We'll go back to the hotel so I can take care of you…" he attempted.

I was just about to lose my fucking mind on him when Holly shook her head. "No, I think I need to be on my own."

"Actually, with a head injury, my medical suggestion is for you to be watched at all times. Even if you didn't pass out, you were hit pretty hard and that's a nasty bump. I need someone to keep an eye on you all night, waking you every two hours to ensure you don't have a concussion. Unless of course you're amenable to going to the hospital and being checked…"

"Jesus, this situation is getting worse by the minute, Colin," said a dark-haired woman I hadn't seen before. She was wearing a black satin strapless gown. "We've already got the press all over the woman attacking your date and then you being tackled by your security team while women act like piranhas having just been fed a juicy steak for the first time. We have to get on top of this. You don't have the time to play nursemaid to some gold-digger," she snapped.

"Who the fuck are you?" I stood, putting myself between Holly and this bitch.

"I'm Carmen Deetz, his manager. You must be the date's security. Can you get her out of here without anyone seeing her?"

"Gladly," I rumbled as Holly stood and put her hands on my back.

"Bruno, please don't make the situation worse," Holly pleaded in a low whiney voice I hated.

I changed the subject. "You said there was a back private entrance?"

"Carmen, I need to make sure Holly's okay. She's my date, and this is all my fault," Colin explained.

"No, you need to get out there, make sure you've met the expectations of your movie producers by making a speech, donating a million dollars to the charity you chose, and soaking up all the good press. You need it more now, after that debacle out front." Carmen glanced at me and then at Holly. "Besides, it looks like she's being taken care of just fine to me."

"Agreed," I shifted to put my arm around Holly. "Let's get you settled in our room where I can keep an eye on you."

"Our room?" Colin blurted. "I booked you a separate one on the floor below us."

"Yeah, that's not going to work for me. Read your contract. Security stays in the same suite, or in this case, room, as the candidate."

"Candidate?" Carmen asked.

"You're her security guy, not her boyfriend. Don't you think that's overdoing it a bit?"

"After what you just put her through, I'm not about to take any chances with her life. And since you just put her on the media's radar, and that of your deranged fans, the closer I am to Holly, the better. Now get out of my way."

"Bruno…" Holly dug her nails into my bicep. "Don't be rude."

"This is me being nice," I snapped and dragged her past an agitated Colin, who was raking his fingers through his hair and looking at Holly as though she was his long-lost puppy. One that had somehow found a new owner.

"I'll call you when this is over, Holly, I swear. We'll work it out!" Colin called out.

"Don't hold your fucking breath," I grumbled as I followed the hotel attendant to a back exit. There was a shiny black limo already waiting.

I scanned the street and was relieved when I didn't see a single photographer. Quickly, I hustled Holly into the limo, slid in beside her, and told the driver to get the hell out of dodge.

We were off without anyone being the wiser.

Chapter 12

Bacon Cheeseburgers and Home Alone

HOLLY

My forehead throbbed so hard I swore I could feel the beat within my eyes. Bruno hadn't said a word on the limo ride back to the hotel. Fury pumped off his frame in tsunami level tidal waves. I was almost nervous to interrupt the cataclysmic brood he was stewing in, for fear of him going off like a volcano blast, but that wasn't who we were. We would be talking about all of this, but I, too, needed some quiet time to pour through my feelings on all that occurred.

When we made it to the room Colin had reserved for me, Bruno didn't ask to stay. He simply ushered me inside and locked the door. I ignored him, found the shopping bags Colin had left for me with essentials, and slipped into the bathroom. I pawed through the items finding a dress for tomorrow, a make-up kit from some designer I'd never heard of, likely because I bought my makeup at Target, and sandals. Another smaller bag held a brand-new bra and panty set. When I thought about it, buying lingerie for someone you haven't even kissed yet was rather weird.

What I didn't find was anything to wear to bed.

"Fuck my life," I groaned out loud, frustration leaking into the very air I breathed.

"What's wrong? Are you in pain?" The bathroom door opened instantly, no knock, no nothing. The man had serious boundary issues.

I rolled my eyes but even that hurt. I covered my forehead lightly with one hand, glad to feel that the bump had receded substantially due to the ice I'd held to it the entire ride over.

"Colin didn't buy me anything to wear to bed," I sighed.

"Of course he didn't. Probably hoping you'd be naked and in his bed," he snapped.

"Are you going to be this pissy all evening? If so, I'd be more comfortable if you just left."

"Not happening," he said while shucking off his suit jacket. He tossed it to a chair then yanked out the bottom of his shirt from where it was tucked into his pants.

I stared rapt, as he started to unbutton his shirt.

"Uh…what are you doing?" I swallowed against the sudden dryness in my throat.

He tilted his head as he finished undoing the last button and shrugged off the shirt, the fabric falling away from his frame to where he held onto it with one finger. Then he passed the item to me.

"For bed," he offered.

I snatched the shirt, desperately trying not to drool over his beautiful bare chest. It was even better with all the lights on. So many hills and valleys, tight flexing muscles…

"At least I know you still like my body," he flaunted.

"Don't be stupid. You know you look amazing. Humble doesn't suit you," I spat before turning around and slamming the bathroom door in his perfect fucking face.

The laughter coming through the closed door made me want to smack him and kiss him again.

"Holly, you are so fucked up," I whispered to my reflection, wincing as the wound on my forehead was already turning a light shade of purple. The center of the injury was still swollen and painful to the touch.

What was I going to do about Colin?

Scratch that, what the hell was I going to do about this living breathing thing between Bruno and me?

I would agree that the sexual attraction was off the charts. Every sexual experience with him was fostering this carnal seed inside me to bloom. It was as if I had a sexy vixen hidden within me and was single-handedly bringing her to the surface, in spades. Worse is, I like that side of myself. The wild sex, and the way I lose myself to him and the connection between us was unbelievably freeing. I honestly didn't know that side of me existed, but I've come to like her, and what Bruno and I shared, more than I wanted to admit.

And what was with him continuing to flirt, entice, and antagonize me?

He claimed earlier that I was giving him mixed signals, but he's the one that keeps setting me aflame through his lust-filled gaze, his not so innocent touches, and the way he blatantly brought up chocolate cake earlier? He knew exactly what he was doing, reminding me of that debauched, exceptionally hot sex we'd had. But why?

No strings is no strings.

Right?

Could he honestly want more with me?

I shook my head and winced at the jarring bolt of pain. I hissed through my teeth as I removed the stunning dress I'd never wear again and put on Bruno's dress shirt over my panties. The ends fell to my thigh but I'm not sure why I cared, because Bruno had seen it all and then some.

After I'd gently washed my face, I pulled my hair into a light bun on the top of my head and exited the bathroom.

Bruno was bare-footed, bare-chested and wearing nothing but dress slacks. He looked good enough to eat. Which was the exact moment my stomach grumbled. I hadn't had anything since the protein bar the glam team handed me earlier that day.

"I'm starving," Bruno announced.

"Well, you're not going down on me right now, so forget about it Mister!" I snapped and then glared as I walked to the closet to hang the dress.

Bruno chuckled. "I meant for food, but I'm always down for a little dessert when you're ready."

"Do you ever stop?" I returned.

His eyebrow cocked. "Do you really want me to?"

I actually didn't want him to stop. I enjoyed our banter almost more than the sex…almost. But even under extreme duress I would never admit it.

"I'm hungry too. Can you order me a bacon cheeseburger, fries and a Coke? And if they have some whiskey, I wouldn't be mad at that either."

"You want a burger, fries, and a coke?" He repeated, sounding shocked.

"*Bacon cheeseburger,*" I enunciated. "Don't forget the *bacon* or the *cheese* or there will be consequences."

He grinned and leaned against the dresser. "I'd like to see what those consequences might be. More importantly, will we be naked for them?"

I closed my eyes, fisted my hands and growled. "I swear to God," I was about to nail him right to the wall.

"Okay, okay," he held his hands up in supplication while chuckling. "I'm sorry. I'm just trying to get your goat and help you forget about today."

I frowned. "That's kinda nice actually," I pouted and then

went over to the big fluffy bed and slowly crawled from the foot up to the headboard.

"If you're going to wave that fine ass in my face, I can't promise to be a gentleman," he croaked.

I turned my head to look over my shoulder and realized my position. Up on all fours with my ass waving in the air just as he claimed.

I shifted to my bum on the coverlet as fast as possible. "That wasn't intentional."

"Noted. Don't worry. I'll be a good boy. You don't need sex right now. You need food, water, these pills," he shook out four two-hundred-milligram Ibuprofen from a bottle the doctor must have given him, "and rest."

He grabbed a bottle of water from the small bar and handed it and the pills to me. "You take those, I'm going to order our food and then go fill the ice bucket so I can make you a new ice pack. Doc handed me a note that said intermittent icing along with the pills before we left."

I took the pills and snuggled under the blankets, the smell of leather mixed liberally with bergamot and a scent that could only be uniquely Bruno, filled my nose. I breathed it in deeply and closed my eyes. "I'll be here," I mumbled, letting the day disappear while I relaxed.

All too soon there was a knock on the door.

"What…who is it?" I muttered, pushing myself to sit back against the headboard.

"The food," Bruno said and disappeared behind a little wall to open the door. I could hear him talking quietly to someone and then he appeared pushing a food cart into the bedroom.

"How long have I been out?" I asked, my gaze on the two bacon cheeseburgers that appeared when Bruno lifted the lids. My mouth watered at the sight of all that goodness.

"You've been crashed out the last hour. I waited to order the food so you could get a good nap in. How do you feel?" He asked while he prepped my plate, and silverware, then brought it over to me. I sat cross-legged and put my plate down on my lap, grabbing a French fry and shoving it in my mouth. It was nice and hot and salted to perfection.

I hummed while I chewed. "Better now. My head hurts less. The meds and nap really did help. Thank you, Bruno," I looked to the side, not making eye contact. "For, taking care of me. For everything. You were there for me today, and it could have gotten really bad."

He came and sat down next to my legs, then reached for my knee and squeezed. "Holly, look at me," he asked gently.

I lifted my gaze and saw nothing but his concern. The broody alpha hot guy was gone and left behind was just Bruno. A good man that didn't want to see me hurt.

"You will always be my priority," he stated like a vow.

My bottom lip trembled. "It could have been so much worse today. Those women, that scene…" my voice trembled. "It reminded me of when the brothers attacked me last week."

He nodded and rubbed my leg. "I feared it might. I'm sorry too."

"For fingering me in the bathroom?"

He grinned wickedly and shook his head. "I'll never be sorry for that."

"For being a grumpy asshole to Colin?" My eyebrows rose, wondering if I was warm or cold.

"Again, no."

"For flirting with me nonstop." I picked up a French fry and ate it.

He chuckled.

"For…"

"Holly baby, stop talking."

"Well now you should be sorry for that because…rude!" I grumbled.

Bruno's head dropped as he half-sighed half-laughed.

"You're going to be the death of me," his sparkling brown eyes found mine. "But what a way to go."

I shoved at his shoulder. "Shut up. I believe you were apologizing to me…"

"I'm sorry I didn't get to you before you got hit by that deranged fan. I should have clocked that wacko, but it's a new type of threat I wasn't expecting. I haven't had experience protecting celebrities. My work usually deals with corporate security, extractions, government contracts and a whole host of activities that walk the line of being legal. Colin's guards said the event was safe on the way over. Promised me up and down that the event had a surplus of security. I trusted them." His mouth twisted into a grimace. "I shouldn't have. There is no world in which you should be getting hurt when I'm within ten feet of you. That will never happen again. I swear on my life, Holly."

"Whoa, whoa, whoa, what happened to me is not on you. They should have been better prepared. You saved me."

He looked away, seemingly not able to look me in the eye. I reached over my plate and put my hand to his cheek. "It's your turn to look at me, Mister."

I could see his jaw firm as he clenched his teeth. A dark lock of hair curled over his forehead as he turned his head to face me, making him seem boyish and younger than his thirty-four years. It did not, however, distract me from how handsome he was.

"None of this is on you. Please listen to me when I say this. None of what happened to me is your fault. You're the only person that has been in my corner through all of it. Thank you for taking care of me. I feel safe when I'm with you. You give that to me, and the only people that ever made me feel secure have been my parents. So, thank you, Bruno."

He gave a solemn tip of his lips. "We should eat."

"Oh my God, yes we should!" I picked up my burger and took a monster bite.

"Damn girl, you sure can eat. I'm used to women ordering salads and picking at their food. You eat with gusto." He reached out and booped the tip of my nose. "I like it. You're honest. In a town full of a whole lot of fake, you're the real deal, Holly Knight."

He got up and brought a Coke over and set it on my end table. There was a little bottle of Maker's Mark right next to it. "You get one for now. I'm not sure it's a good idea to drink after a head injury, so take it easy."

"'K," I mumbled around my food. Then he went and got his own plate and fully loaded whiskey, again rude, before coming back to settle on the other side of the bed. He reached for the remote and turned on the TV.

A movie I recognized and loved appeared on the screen. "Ohhh *Home Alone!* This movie is awesome, have you seen it?"

He smiled and nodded. "It's one of my favorites," he admitted.

For the next hour and a half, we watched Kevin and his shenanigans against the robbers trying to get into his house. We laughed at the same parts, even mimicking the dialogue in the same places. It was really nice.

When it finished, Bruno took our plates and pushed the food cart into the hallway then turned off all the lights. I watched through the glow from the TV as he unzipped and removed his pants, letting them fall to the floor. I couldn't help but sneak a peek of his body in a pair of well-fitting black boxer briefs, because damn, he had it going on. Thankfully, he didn't do anything but slide into bed.

"Come here, Holly." He reached for me.

I scooted over to his side and cuddled against his chest.

White Christmas with Bing Crosby and Rosemary Clooney came on next.

"I used to watch this with my parents every year when I was growing up. Mom loves musicals. Have you seen this one?"

I asked.

"Nope. I can't say that musicals are on my list of favorites, but I'm willing to give it a shot for you."

I tunneled my fingers into his chest hair and sighed. "What do you normally do for Christmas?"

"If I'm not on a case, or traveling, I usually spend it with Joel and his daughter Penny and my aunt Olympia. Joel's my first cousin, but now that he's remarried to Faith, who also has a daughter, Eden, I don't want to intrude. And besides, I'll be here this year, watching you get engaged."

"Engaged," I repeated, having trouble believing it myself. "Do you think Colin's still interested in me after everything?" My voice was small and more insecure than I would have liked, but I needed a man's opinion.

"Oh, he's interested. The real question is, are you?"

"Does it really matter? The bidder gets to decide…"

His hold tightened around me. "That's not exactly true. I've read the contracts forward and backward. Even if he bids on you and wins, you still have the ability to say no. You have the final say by signing the contract or not. Nothing goes through if you don't sign on the dotted line at the end of the auction."

"I need the money."

"I know," he sighed.

"I want to take care of my family. I want to be the one to make my dreams come true. And today, Colin just offered to hand it all to me on a silver platter."

"And then you had a panic attack," he oh so helpfully reminded me. "That says a lot without saying anything."

"Yeah," I admitted on a soft whisper.

"What if someone like me offered you the money?" His tone was searching, holding a hint of nervous energy.

"I can't take your money. I won't. Then it's you paying my way instead of Colin. There's no difference," I harrumphed.

"Not *take*, loan. You said before you would be doing this

all yourself if the bank loaned you the money. What if I had my lawyers set up a contract for the loan? With say, 1% interest with an unlimited term on paying me back in the agreement. You can pay when you can pay."

"Ugh," I covered my eyes. "It's the same thing. A man handing me my dreams."

"I don't want to watch you marry another man, Holly, but I will if that's what you want."

The room in the air became thick as molasses as so much was insinuated without admitting the truth of what was happening between us. We were entering uncharted territory, and I wasn't sure how to best wade through the murky waters without losing everything.

"What do you want?" I asked.

"I don't know. This. Lying in bed watching Christmas movies with you. Insanely good sex. Endless bickering. Messy bacon cheeseburgers and chocolate cake," he waggled his brows. "But the truth is, I'm not the type of guy that can settle down. Not traditionally. My work is important to me. And it's dangerous. Sometimes I'm gone a few days, a week, a month, or longer when I'm on a difficult job. That's not fair to you or any woman. It never has been before."

"Makes sense why you're so standoffish."

"Standoffish? I thought I was broody?" he teased.

"You're that too." I snickered. "It just so happens I like all of it."

He shifted his head and kissed me lightly on the forehead. "I like you too."

"What happens next?"

He shook his head as my eyes felt heavy, the food, the warmth, the Christmas music lulling me into a serene space that had me drifting.

"Whatever is meant to be, will be." I felt another feather-light kiss, this time on my forehead as sleep stole me away.

Chapter 13

A Lump of Coal

BRUNO

An incessant buzzing noise roused me from the best sleep I'd had in years. I stretched out my hand to quiet my phone when a loud trill sounded across the room, coming from Holly's purse.

"Shit," I grumbled as Holly moaned in her sleep, repositioned her thigh that was curled over my leg, her arm hugging my chest. Her head was tucked against my shoulder, the silky strands of her hair shifting like satin ribbons teasing along my bare skin.

"Huh, what…what's happening?" she croaked, her tone thick with sleep.

"Our phones are going off," I groaned as she moved so that I could reach mine.

The display screen showed it was Alana calling.

"Fuck," I let out a sharp breath and hit the answer button. "Hello?"

Holly shimmied out of my hold and crawled to her phone. Before she could reach it, a knock pounded on the door.

"Mr. Castellanos, it is Alana Toussaint," my caller announced.

"Yeah, Alana, I know who it is," I shucked off the covers and walked toward the door as Holly answered her phone. I glanced at the clock. "It's seven in the morning. Why are you calling so early?"

"Mom? What? No...I'm okay. Yeah, I'm fine. You saw what on TV?" she murmured as I made my way sleepily to the door and to the nonstop knocking.

"Care to explain to me why I'm watching my candidate be man-handled and bludgeoned on national television?" Alana's clipped tone revealed her fury.

"I'm sorry, what are you talking about?" I frowned and blinked a few times, trying to dispel the sleep still clinging to my consciousness.

"Are you going to tell me Holly and Colin weren't attacked on the red-carpet last night? Because I assure you, the millions of photographs and videos that are all over the news, the internet, and social media, paint a pretty damning picture."

The pounding at the door continued. "Hold on a moment. Someone's at the door."

"Mr. Castellanos, I want some answers," Alana demanded as I opened the door.

Colin stopped mid-knock, his gaze traveling down my unclothed form and messy bedhead. I smiled like the cat that ate up all the cream.

"I'm sorry, I thought this was Holly's room. I apologize for disturbing you," he rushed to course correct.

"No, she's here." I let the door go and walked away, letting

Colin choose to come in or not. He followed me in.

Holly was pacing the floor in front of the bed, wearing nothing but my dress shirt.

"Mom, I swear to God, I am fine. I'll be home today. Yes, we can meet for dinner. No, I already went to the doctor's. Yes, I was seen by a real doctor. I didn't call you because I knew you'd overreact..."

"Holly, you have company," I announced like the asshole I was.

Colin stopped in the middle of the small living space and stared at Holly. I was not prepared for how crestfallen his expression would be when he saw the two of us, neither wearing appropriate clothing.

"I came to check on you..." he pointed at her and then at me. "Obviously you've been taken great care of. I'll just go."

"Colin," she reached out her hand, "No. Please. I can explain."

"Why you just crawled out of bed with your bodyguard? Save it." He bit out angrily.

"Mom, I have to go," Holly said as Alana's voice rose in my ear.

"Are you listening? You. Are. Fired. Mr. Castellanos. Escort Holly home and I'll pay you for your services to date, but our contract moving forward is terminated." Alana snapped.

"Whoa, whoa, whoa. You're firing me?" I scoffed.

"*Oui!* We'll discuss more in person," Alana stated flatly and then hung up.

"I can't believe she fired me," I chuckled. I'd never been fired from any job in my life.

"She's firing you!" Holly cried.

"I'm outta here," Colin said, shaking his head.

"No!" Holly chased after him, gripping his wrist while still holding onto her phone. "This isn't what it seems. I didn't sleep with him. Well, I mean, I did sleep with him, but only to *sleep*!"

she attempted to placate the actor, while I did my best not to laugh. This whole scenario was right out of a comedy movie.

"So, you're telling me you're not fucking your bodyguard?" Colin deadpanned.

"I…I didn't have sex with him last night," she responded, failing miserably at hiding the real truth.

"As opposed to another night. Don't be coy with me. Three's a crowd, Holly. And you're wearing his shirt and are perfectly comfortable standing in a room where he's only in his underwear. That speaks of a level of intimacy beyond the scope of professionalism."

He had her there. I crossed my arms over my bare chest and leaned against the back of the small couch, watching the show.

"But…"

He shook his head. "My jet will take you and your *bodyguard*, or whatever the fuck he is, back to Las Vegas in two hours. Be ready or fly commercial. Frankly, I no longer care. And to think, I was worried about you and the media coverage. I shouldn't have. It looks like you can take care of yourself just fine without me." He growled and stormed out of the room.

Holly put the phone back up to her ear. "I gotta go, Mom. I'll see you at dinner. Yes, I swear I'll be there. I love you too. Bye." She said and then hung up. The phone fell to the floor as her hands came up to cover her eyes. Her body bowed forward as the sobs started.

"Oh baby, no…" I went over to her, planning to console her. Instead, she screeched and shoved me away.

"Don't touch me," she seethed. "That's how all of this got so messed up in the first place."

"Are you saying you regret our time together?" I raged on the inside. What I've shared with Holly has been more special than any relationship I've had in a long time. I was even starting to imagine a different world, one in which I could have the love of a good woman in my life, and maybe a real home to go to after a job ended, instead of a mostly empty loft I rented in New York.

She ripped her hands through her hair and held the mass on top of her head, tears streaming down her botchy red cheeks. "We fucked it all up. Now Colin doesn't want me. You don't want me. The banks don't fucking want me. And when we go back to Alana's office, she's probably going to let me go too, and then what? I'm back at square one all over again."

"Holly, we'll figure it out. I'll help make it right."

"By what? Offering me the money again? Making my mother less afraid her daughter's going to end up killed by some deranged person? Because that shit is real, Bruno, and it's happened to me twice in the past two weeks. Or maybe you can fix it all by sexing me up some more. You know, making me lose my mind and my good sense!" She let her hair fall in waves over her shoulders while her hands went behind the back of her head. "Please, for the love of God, tell me how you are going to fix this disaster? Because things are looking pretty freakin' bleak right about now!"

I lifted my hands into a prayer position and lowered my tone. "I agree. But there's always a way. I just need you to trust me. Okay? Trust that I have your best interest at heart and will find a way to smooth everything over. Let's just get dressed, catch the plane back to Vegas, and I'll work my magic. Okay?"

She was about to speak when I lifted a finger for her to pause. "Trust me."

Holly closed her eyes, inhaled fully, let it out slowly and nodded once. "I can be ready to go in fifteen minutes. Do you want the shower first?" she offered.

"We could take a shower together to save time…" I lowered my voice suggestively.

"Are you fucking kidding me right now?" she snapped.

I grinned. "Just trying to lighten up the situation. Man.

Tough crowd. Why don't you shoot a man already."

"Give me your gun and let's see what happens?"

Damn she was a spitfire. I loved every second of it. "I'll go first. I only need five minutes."

"Fine," she glared.

"Fine," I chuckled and sauntered past her, pushing my briefs down as I did so, making sure she got a nice view of my bare ass.

Her reaction was a little gasp that I knew she was trying to cover. That small kernel of hope and continued attraction meant I still had her on my hook. It lifted my spirits instantly.

I'd fix everything. I was certain of it. I just needed to figure out a solid plan, and I had a handful of hours to do it.

Piece of cake.

Just not a piece of chocolate cake.

At least it was better than a lump of coal, which was what I was looking at if I didn't make things right for Holly and with Madam Alana.

Chapter 14

Holy Night

HOLLY

My life had gone to hell in a handbasket. The confident, driven woman I was two weeks ago, before all of this, was gone. The woman left behind was a confused, sullen mess. I needed to get my shit together. Everything had changed after I'd been attacked by the Baskin brothers, but it wasn't just them. It was Bruno. All of this back and forth, the fighting, the fucking, the trying to keep things to just sex, with no strings, was all a big fat lie. I'd fallen in love with the asshole, and it was destroying my life.

For thirty years I'd done my thing. Hooked up with men when I needed. Went on dates if I felt lonely, but not a single man stuck. There wasn't another man I wanted to be connected to every single day of my life…until now. And he didn't do traditional. Before meeting him, I wouldn't have thought I did the traditional relationship either, but somehow, he'd wormed his way under my skin and became a part of me that I didn't want to live without.

Now, I needed to break it off with him.

I was working up the courage to end things when we got off the elevator on the floor where The Marriage Auction was headquartered.

Not being able to hold off a second longer I reached for his wrist and tugged him to a quiet corner. He turned around and tilted his head, his brow furrowing.

"You're finally going to speak to me?" he asked.

We'd just spent the last few hours in complete silence. After we both took a shower, *individually* I might add, back in LA, we'd boarded Colin's jet and came straight here as requested. I'd been entirely lost within my own thoughts, but now, I had something to say.

"Before we go in there, I just need to tell you…regardless of everything that happened, I don't regret you or what we shared. I've learned a lot about myself. Sexually, emotionally, and mentally. You've been a safe space for me, and I thank you for that."

"Holly, I'm sorry. For everything bad that's happened to you. I promised I'd make it right with Alana and I will," he pushed.

I shook my head. "That's just it. I don't need you to fight my battles for me, Bruno. I will discuss the situation regarding my inclusion in the auction with her privately. I'd encourage you to do the same regarding your security contract."

"I don't give a shit about the contract. The money she's paying me is a pittance to what I normally bring in for a month of work. I was originally doing it as a favor to my cousin, Joel."

I shrugged. "Well, there you go. Now you can leave free

and clear. Go back to your big-money, dangerous deals and leave all of this behind."

He frowned. "What are you saying, Holly? Are you breaking it off with me?"

"Am I ending our nonexistent relationship?" I gave a half-hearted chuckle even though the truth was eating me alive.

I wanted more than what we had, far more, but he made it clear he wasn't the type of guy who made any long-term commitments. Long distance I could do with a partner. I didn't need a man at my beck and call, or even in my world every single day. I still had my dream of opening my own bar and hiring my family to help run it. That hadn't changed. How I'd get there may ultimately change, depending on what Alana said after the meeting. But I'd made it clear that I wasn't the type of woman to tie a man down. I'd even shared a fantasy with Bruno of my man coming home from a long trip away and shagging me in my pretend dream office. He obviously didn't see himself in that role, so what was a woman in my position to do?

Bruno hadn't said a single word that would lead me to believe he wanted a forever type of love or any kind of love at all. I wasn't sure he even knew how to give that part of himself. I'd seen glimpses of it, when he was taking care of me, or helping me down from that panic attack, but was that love? It felt close, but we both had the contract looming to fall back on. Not to mention the knowledge that it would all end at some point. Sure, he'd said he didn't want to watch me marry someone else, but he didn't offer to be that man either.

"I wouldn't say what we have is nonexistent," he responded. "I can very clearly remember pounding you against the shower, the bed, the…"

I held up my hand to stop him. "Please, don't remind me."

He reached out and took my hand. "Holly, come on. This is ridiculous. We know what we have."

"Correction, had. We know what we *had*, Bruno. It's all

gone up in flames. Actually, *my life* has all gone up in flames. Nothing in yours has changed at all. I need to reassess and figure out how I'm going to put the pieces all back together."

"And what about us?"

"What about us? You don't do traditional relationships and I'm about to go in there and beg Alana not to let me go. I let this thing between us get out of hand. Took my eyes off the prize, which was stupid. So stupid of me."

"Now you're saying what we had was stupid? And you're ready to throw it all away and put your hat back into the marriage auction ring just like that." His expression was filled with shock, something I didn't expect.

I stepped closer and placed my hands on his chest. "What we had was magical, intense, and brutally honest. It was also wildly inappropriate under the circumstances. And yet, I don't regret it. As a matter of fact, I love what we shared, got completely lost in it, and even fell in love with you in the process. But we're at the point where we both need to do what's best for ourselves."

"You're telling me you're in love with me, but you're going to marry someone else." His voice was like sandpaper over rock. Wounded and scarred raw.

"That's exactly what I'm telling you." I cupped his cheeks, lifted up onto my toes, and placed my mouth over his. I'd planned it to be a sweet goodbye kiss, but he took it to a whole new level.

His tongue plunged into my mouth, and he devoured me whole. I gave back all that I could, sucking at his tongue, nipping at his bottom lip, then kissing it better. His hands ran along my frame as though he owned me, and I allowed it…this one final time. As we kissed, I imprinted the memory of his lips against mine, the minty flavor of his breath, the heated growl he gave as he swallowed my whimpers. I never wanted to forget being desired this much and wanting the same in return.

We finally pulled away, both of us panting.

"Even after that, you're going to walk in there and ask her to keep you in the auction?" he growled, fury and disappointment flooding his features.

"Are you offering me something different?" I looked at him with all the hope and love filling my heart. All he had to do was reach for it and take hold and never let go.

"I-I told you I'd give you the money." Fire laced through my gut and must have shown on my face because he instantly corrected his statement. "I meant *loan* you the money."

I closed my eyes and shook my head. He didn't get it and he never would. "It's not about the money anymore, Bruno. And the fact that you think it is, is the real problem. I'll find a way to make my dreams come true if the auction thing is no longer on the table. I'm a strong, independent, intelligent woman. I'm fully capable of pivoting and changing direction. What I'm not capable of is being in a physical relationship with you, without more."

"What more do you want?" he pleaded, his voice strained.

"Strings. Attachment. A *real* relationship. One filled with love, support, and commitment."

"I don't even know what that means or what something like that would look like," he admitted, his shoulders falling in defeat. "It's not in my nature…"

I gave him a weak smile. "And that's why this thing between us needs to end here." I patted his chest and looked deeply into his eyes. "I love you, Bruno. You deserve happiness. True happiness. I hope you find it someday."

And with tears in my eyes, I left him standing there as I approached Jade, Alana's assistant. "I believe Alana wants to see me," I swallowed down the heartache, lifted my chin, and reset my intention.

"Right this way," Jade stood and gestured to the set of double doors down the hall.

I glanced over my shoulder to find Bruno still there, his tortured gaze on me. "Goodbye, Bruno." I said and then followed Jade.

"First and foremost, *chérie*, are you okay?" Alana winced as she looked at the black, blue, and green, bruise on my forehead. Most of the swelling had gone down but it did look pretty ugly.

I moved to touch it, then remembered how tender it was. "I'll be fine. I'm not going to lie; it was pretty scary. I can't imagine how anyone could live like that day after day. Did um, Colin have anything to share about it?"

"He did." Alana said without a hint of what was said between them.

"I see. Does this mean I'm out of the auction?" Guilt and shame ate at my insides and my palms became clammy, ready for Alana to bring down the gauntlet.

Alana put her elbows to her desk, interlaced her fingers, and rested her chin on top of them. I waited for the bomb to drop.

"Why would you think I'm removing you from the auction? Does this have to do with Mr. Castellanos being fired? His egregious error in protecting you doesn't reflect on your status within my company."

"I'm sorry..." my mouth fell open in shock. "Did Colin speak with you? About what happened?"

"Of course, *chérie*. He did so when he pulled himself out of the bidding pool. Claimed his lifestyle was too dangerous for one of my candidates. He said he needed someone who knew the business and pitfalls of being with a celebrity. I'm going to have another meeting with him in the coming weeks to suggest a private auction and ensure that I will line up clients that are aware of the pros and cons of marrying a man of his caliber and fame."

He didn't say anything about finding Bruno and me together in a compromising position.

"Colin is a saint," I gasped.

"Aw, that's sweet, darling. Are you disappointed he won't be bidding on you?" Her tone was concerned and completely unnecessary.

I shook my head. "Um, no. I'm just glad I'm still in the running."

Alana smiled. "Me too. I wanted to see you today to not only make sure you were truly okay, but to tell you that I've terminated our contract with Mr. Castellanos' firm. You will have a new bodyguard assigned for your next set of dates. If you are amenable, we'll start them back-to-back for the next couple weeks. I didn't want to say before, but many of my bidders chose you for a date prior to the auction."

"Wow," my heart sank while thoughts of Bruno twisted in my gut painfully. "That's…great. When can we start?" I sighed and plastered on my fakest smile.

"Tomorrow evening. Rest tonight and meet me in the lobby bar tomorrow at six p.m. I'll introduce you to your next bidder. If you need help covering that bruise, I can have our glam team see you at five."

I nodded. "Thank you, Alana. I won't let you down."

What I really wanted to say was, I won't let me down.

Now if my heart and my brain could work together, all would be well.

Chapter 15

All I Want for Christmas is You

BRUNO

Two weeks later…

It was Christmas Eve. The night of the auction. I had no doubt Holly would be chosen. I wasn't proud of it, but I'd had Jonas do his thing and hack Alana's systems. Holly had gone out on eight dates in the past two weeks. I had eyes on the most notable ones. There was an oil tycoon that wore a cowboy hat in every picture of him on the internet. That told me the man was bald under that hat, but he didn't have any red flags. Then, of course, there was a restauranteur, a hotelier, a real estate magnate, and a whole laundry list of other "respectable" men, all vying for Holly's attention. All healthy options on paper for my girl.

My girl, I huffed.

What the fuck did that even mean anymore? Holly wasn't *my* anything.

No, that wasn't true.

Holly was my *everything*. She was the one that got away. The loss of my life. The one woman on the entire planet that seemed to love me, assholery be damned. She didn't care that I was crass or bossy or that I liked control in the bedroom. Holly dove right into the deep end with me, treaded water and howled at the moon gleefully. I'd never had that before and I wouldn't ever have it again.

She put all of her cards on the table, and I let her go.

She loves me and I let her go.

Correction. She *loved* me.

And I'd spent the last two weeks stewing in everything we'd shared, and all that she said. Not knowing the first thing on how to deal with the complicated feelings I had over losing her. This was not a typical scenario for me. I didn't know the best way to get past what kept coming to the surface every time I allowed a memory of our time together to invade my mind.

Whiskey and Coke.

Shower sex.

Chocolate-coated kisses.

Sleepy morning sex.

Sparkly green dresses.

Airplane bathrooms.

Bacon cheeseburgers

Home Alone.

And the worst, the absolute fucking worst memory that played on repeat like a broken record was the way she looked at me after she was attacked. Like her *savior*. As though I personally had hung the moon so it could shine just for her.

She said she loved me.

Holly Knight looked into my eyes and told me that she had fallen in love with me. And what did I do?

Nothing.

No, I did do something.

I walked away.

I clenched my teeth until they ached, lifted the whiskey to my mouth and let the anger burn through my system along with two fingers worth of an eighteen-year-old bottle of Macallan.

Did I love her?

"Fuck yes! I'm in love with her." I slammed the glass down so hard on the glossy bar top I heard the tumbler crack.

But what was I to do about it? She was getting ready right now, in this very hotel, to walk across that stage and offer herself up to the highest bidder. All because I wasn't able to get my head out of my ass and tell her how I felt.

"Sir, are you okay?" the bartender asked, gesturing to where my hands were white knuckled around the empty tumbler.

"No, I'm not okay. I'm about to lose the love of my life forever."

The man tossed his towel over one shoulder, braced his hands on the bar top and leaned forward as though he had a secret to share or some wisdom to impart.

"Well, what are you going to do about it? Sit here and drink yourself into oblivion on Christmas Eve?"

I shook my head and waited for him to continue.

"Go after her, dummy."

A gruff, dry laugh left me. "Just like that?"

He shrugged a shoulder and then pried the glass from my hand. "What's the worst that could happen? You lose her again? The only thing you know right now for sure is that you'll definitely lose her if you do nothing but sit here and bury your sorrows in a three-hundred-and-fifty-dollar bottle of whiskey."

Wild, untamed thoughts raced through my mind. If I wanted to prove that I was serious about Holly, and having a real relationship with her, I needed to take the leap. Not only tell her how I felt but *show* her with my actions.

I grinned and stood. "You're a fucking genius," I pulled out my wallet and laid down ten one-hundred-dollar bills. "Keep the change my friend. And thank you!"

"Invite me to the wedding!" he called out as I stormed out of the lobby bar and to the elevator that led to the ballroom where they were hosting the auction.

When the elevator opened, I set off at a dead run, knowing the auction had already started. I had to hope the universe, God, karma, Aphrodite, or whatever deity was watching right now, that I'd make it in time.

As I approached, Jade stood at the door, her phone to her ear. Her eyes widened at the picture I must have presented. I'm sure I looked awful, in a wrinkled all-black suit, whiskey breath, sweat misting along my hairline making my hair curl even more out of control than normal.

Her hands rose to stop me from entering. "This is a private event, Mr. Castellanos."

"Jade, you have to let me in," I barked, then bent over and sucked in several lungsful of air. My heartbeat was a bass drum against my chest and my mouth dry as the desert.

"I will call security..."

"Please, you don't understand. I need to talk to Holly. I have to tell her."

"Holly is next on stage. Whatever you have to say to her needs to wait until the auction has finished..."

"It will be too late!" I shouted and moved to the door. I'd just curled my hand around the golden lever when Jade pushed her body in front of me. "Jade, you need to move. I have to tell Holly how I feel. I'm in love with her. She can't marry another man. I want her to marry me!"

"You're what?" she whisper-gasped. "When did that happen?"

"For fuck's sake woman, we don't have any time!" I pleaded.

"Are you seriously going to bid on her?" she asked as I tugged the door, her body shifting forward enough I heard the dreaded words that could seal my fate, coming through the crack in the door.

"Let's start the bidding at three million dollars," Alana's voice filled the room.

"Yes! Now get outta my way!" I roared, yanked the door hard enough that Jade went stumbling forward, but ultimately caught her balance.

"You're insane!" she hollered.

"I know. I'm sorry. I'll make it up to you!" I swore as I slipped behind the door and into the dark ballroom. There was a shiny black stage set up in the front of the room with bright red poinsettia plants lining the front. A massive screen was lit in the back showing a set of polling results that made my stomach sour instantly.

Holly's name was on the top next to her picture. Underneath that were three lines of text.

Yes = 15

No = 5

Maybe = 10

"I've got three million to bidder number eighteen. Do I have four?"

I scanned the crowd and then the stage. My breath caught when I saw Holly standing near the podium and Alana. She was wearing a dark-green lingerie set. The top was a satin corset. The bottoms were a lacy matching thong. I knew it was a thong because Holly had just turned around and flaunted her juicy ass while looking over her shoulder coyly and blowing a kiss. It reminded me of her wearing my shirt and nothing but panties the last night we had together.

"I have four million to bidder number nine. Do I have five?" Alana cooed, and I followed her gaze to Mr. Cowboy.

"Five million, darlin," he shouted, and the crowd clapped.

"Six million!" I yelled, walking down the center aisle headed toward the stage.

Alana squinted. "I'm sorry Sir, please raise your paddle so I can see your number."

"I don't have a paddle. I don't have a number." I kept walking until I got close enough to the stage that both Holly and Alana could see me clearly. "I don't have anything but the desire to make this woman my wife."

"Bruno," Holly gasped, her hands going to cover her mouth.

"Security!" Alana called out.

"Please don't take me away. I've already screwed everything up. Holly, I love you. I want to marry you. And I will pay six million in order to have that right."

"Seven million!" came a voice in the crowd. One I recognized but didn't believe I'd ever hear again.

"Colin?" Holly's shocked expression matched my own.

The man stood up, his paddle lighting up his face as he grinned wickedly. "I repeat, seven million."

"Eight!" I snapped, fury coiling like a snake in my gut.

"Nine," he crossed his arms over one another and smirked.

"Colin, no. Don't do this. You don't want me. Not really," Holly countered.

"Ten fucking million dollars," I shouted. "I *do* want you, Holly. I'm in love with you and I'm not leaving here without your hand in marriage!"

Security arrived and two burly men hooked their arms with mine.

"Alana, please…I'm in love with her. Allow me to stay. Accept my bid." I fought against the beefy guards. I could have laid them out flat in seconds, but I didn't think that would win me any favors with the Madam, and I was already on her shit list.

"Ma'am?" one of the security guys asked Alana.

Alana turned to Holly who was now standing with tears

streaking down her cheeks.

"Do you want me to allow Bruno to continue?" Alana asked Holly.

Holly's bottom lip trembled then split into a huge smile. My heart swelled with joy and relief.

"I do want him…for ten million dollars," she laughed heartily, and the flood of relief almost buckled my knees.

"He can stay." Alana informed her guards and they let me go. But she wasn't done. "Mr. Omstead, you said you weren't bidding tonight, just entertaining the process. Did you want to counter bid?" she asked, and it took everything within my soul to keep my mouth shut. No matter how much money this mother fucker offered, I was going home with Holly, and he was going back to Hollywood.

"No. I just wanted to run the numbers up. Consider it payback." Colin's eyes pierced mine knowingly, and I dipped my head in respect. We'd put the man through the wringer and I welcomed his ire.

"I deserve that, Colin. And thank you, for being a man of honor."

"I'd say it takes one to know one, but we both know I'd be lying. Have a great life. Treat her right."

I turned around and faced Holly. I walked around to the side of the stage, took the steps and stopped in the center before opening my arms. "Come here, Holly!"

Holly bolted across the stage toward me and jumped into the air when she came close enough to reach. I caught her, spun her around and tucked my head into the crook of her neck.

While we held one another the room's lighting lifted, stealing the shadows.

"That concludes our Christmas Auction, and what a showing it was! I hope to see you at the next auction. *Au revoir* and Merry Christmas to you all!"

The sound system came on and Mariah Carey's, "All I want

for Christmas is You" blasted through the speakers.

Holly laughed as I removed my suit jacket and placed it around her, covering her body while she threaded her arms through the sleeves.

She looped her arms around my neck and started to sway to the beat.

"Are you sure you're ready for this?"

"What is this you speak of?" I teased.

"Oh, you know, marriage, date nights, anniversaries, birthdays, my nosey parents, long-distance phone sex, coming-home-from-a-business-trip-away sex. Me working nights at my brand-new bar, when you're back in town." She pressed her lips together then looked at me with those knowing warm eyes I missed so damn much. "None of it will be easy. We'll have to work on it every day."

"Are you up for the challenge of being married to a work-a-holic, broody, overprotective asshole that is emotionally challenged? I may say or do something that will piss you off. I have many priors in pissing you off, as you well know."

She nuzzled against my chest and sighed. "True, but some of that I consider foreplay."

I burst out laughing as we continued to dance on the empty stage.

"I'm sorry about before. I should have told you how I felt."

She tightened her hold around my waist and pressed her head to my heart. "I'm glad you finally did. And if you don't want to get married, we don't have to. I would have dropped out if you'd given me your heart before today. I can figure something else out about the bar."

"Oh no, I bid on you fair and square. You're taking that money. Besides, I don't plan on having a prenuptial agreement. I'm in this with you, Holly. So, half of everything I own will be yours anyway."

"What if I want a prenup for my ten million buck-a-roos?" she clapped back instantly, that fire within her just starting to blaze. "And seriously? Ten million. What were you thinking? You could have had me for *free*. I was ready to jump off the stage the second I saw your face."

I curled my hand around her jaw and tipped her head up toward mine. I kissed her gently, content in the fact that I had the right to do it any time I wanted from here on out.

"How about this? We get married, I invest in *our future* together, by investing in the family business you envision. Besides, I've already started a successful business. I could help. Would that be acceptable?"

She hummed, looking at the ceiling pretending to think about it. "Hmmm, I guess it's not a big deal if my own husband is a silent partner. Emphasis on the silent part."

"Then it's settled. We're getting married and going into business together." I cuddled her close and let everything else fall away. For the first time ever, I was excited about the future and what it might hold.

Mariah's voice rose into the air as the song came to its final crescendo. "You know, this is my new favorite Christmas song," I whispered into her ear.

"Oh yeah?"

"Yeah, because it's true. All I want for Christmas is you, every day, for the rest of our lives."

Epilogue

I'll Be Home for Christmas

HOLLY

One year later...

"Honey, I need a gin and tonic, a glass of the house chardonnay, two shots of Patron, and the Hoot special," my mother slapped her order on the corner of the bar. She wore jeans, and a black t-shirt with the name of my bar, Night Owl, emblazoned across the front in gold lettering. Her shoes were comfy sneakers, and her smile genuine. No more tight skirts or uncomfortable pantyhose for my mama. And Dad, well he rocked shorts, tennis shoes, and a matching t-shirt while working behind the bar. They worked whatever hours they wanted.

I instantly started the shots and prepped the gin and tonic. "Got it, Mom!"

"I've got the chardonnay and the special," Dad hollered, taking half the order. He worked the bar with me most nights, hanging up his card dealing for good, while Mom waitressed whenever she wanted to, which was also most nights. She also loved bossing around the younger cocktail staff and teaching them the ropes.

"Mac says he's got a situation in the parking lot," she added.

"Does he need help?" I asked, finishing up the gin and tonic.

"I sent over one of the brothers," Mom waved her hand, gesturing to one of the VIP sections in the back.

Another change that occurred when I opened up Night Owl was I kept Mac on staff and hired several of his biker buddies for security and bouncing. Bruno demanded he be the one to interview all of them. Turns out, Bruno was most fond of the bikers with records. "Scarier the better, baby. When I'm gone, I want you covered," he'd told me. And since I had been adopted by the Las Vegas Hounds, along with my parents and all of Bruno's guys, my bar was by far the safest place in town.

"What's going on?" Jonas called out with a chin lift, those hawk ears of his hearing all.

"Drama in the parking lot. Mac and his brothers are on it," I responded, setting the drinks on Mom's tray.

Jonas nodded, sipped his beer and put his eyes back on his laptop screens. Jonas had become a regular fixture in mine and my parents' lives too. One of the interesting parts of marrying Bruno was, all of a sudden, I had a brother-in-law of sorts. I almost saw Jonas more than my own husband. Apparently, they never went on the same jobs at the same time, and because Jonas was the tech, he rarely left. Most nights his ass was warming the same seat at my bar. Mom and Dad loved it. He ate dinner with us a couple times a week, watched sports with Dad and had become Mom's personal matchmaking challenge. Every time a beautiful single woman entered the bar and caught her eye, she attempted to introduce her "adopted son" to them. Her words not mine.

My parents had always been the 'more the merrier' type,

and when Bruno suggested this five-story building to not only open Night Owl, but as a place where we could all live, including my parents and his business headquarters, I jumped at the chance. He set it all up while I worked with a designer to create the establishment of my dreams on the bottom level.

The top floor was our five-bedroom home. The fourth floor was halved, one side was my parents two-bedroom apartment, and the other a full gym. Level three was Bruno's headquarters and a two-bedroom apartment that Jonas lived in. Floor two was a set of ten, one-bedroom, decent sized apartments, that Bruno's men rotated in and out of. Many of Bruno's team had homes, wives, husbands, and the like all over the world. When they were in town, he liked having them close so they didn't waste time with unnecessary travel, getting them right back to their families. Some of the men moved in and paid rent because they liked being in Vegas.

Basically, everything had changed for the better once Bruno and I got married on New Year's Eve.

I glanced at the clock above the entrance door right as it struck midnight. It was Christmas Eve, technically now it was Christmas. I watched that clock like my life depended on it waiting for my husband to get back from South America. He and a team of his guys worked some scary ass job he wouldn't tell me much about. But, he promised he would be here for our very first Christmas as husband and wife, and I trusted him to make good on his promise.

And then it happened. The door opened, and a sea of men entered, all wearing black combat-style clothing aside from my man, who was in a black-on-black suit. My mouth watered as I stood there taking in my hot as fuck husband. My heart pounded with excitement as the biggest smile slid across my face. His eyes found mine and our gazes met, as piercing and intense as one year ago today when he dropped all the walls between his heart and mind and took a leap of faith, fighting for my hand in marriage. It was the best day of my life.

I slowly walked down the length of my bar, pushed through the short saloon doors on one end and waited for him to greet me.

When he approached, he bent in half, put his shoulder to my stomach and lifted me up and into a fireman's hold.

"Bruno!" I screeched laughing. "You brute, let me down!"

His hand smacked my ass and then gripped it hard giving it a good jiggle.

"No fucking way. Mom and Dad, I'm taking your daughter for the rest of the night. See you for Christmas brunch?" he called out to my parents.

"Yes, honey! Have fun. Happy you're home safe," my mother called out.

"Mac and I will close down the bar, sweetheart," Dad offered.

"Traitors!" I screeched, playfully smacking my man's rock-hard ass as he dragged me to the back where we had a private elevator only staff used to get to our floors. There was a front entrance that guests could use, but they had to be buzzed in by a 24-hour security guy. Bruno used that job for new recruits of his company and new prospects of the Hounds. They were strict as all get out. No one entered our building unless they lived there, worked for Bruno, or were brought in with one of us. If Bruno had meetings with clients, they were on a list. If they weren't on the list, they didn't get in. Period.

I thought he'd opt for my work office, because it was close, but he carried me straight into the elevator and hit the button for our home. We'd already had sex in my office multiple times over the past year when he'd returned from a job, but for some reason today was different.

The elevator dinged and he carried me straight through the entry, the living room, and down the hall to our bedroom. When we got there, he tossed me on the bed.

"Get naked," he demanded.

I burst into laughter. "You haven't seen me for over two weeks and the first thing you have to say to me is get naked," I giggled.

"Fuck yes," he grouched as he yanked off my shoes and then each sock. "You're the one that sent me a picture of you in that red nightie. It's all I've thought about for five days straight," he bent over my form, lifted my shirt and bit down on my breast over my bra. He palmed them both, then pressed his head between them and sighed.

"Comfy?" I grinned.

"God, yes, this is my happy place," he said, then pressed warm kisses to the fleshy globes, pushed down the lacy cups holding up the girls, and squashed his entire face in between them. He groaned, breathing deeply. "You smell so fucking good, baby," he mumbled against my skin.

"What do I smell like? Sweat and bar stank?" I chuckled.

"No. You smell like home."

I ran my fingers through the curly layers of his hair. "I missed you, Bruno," I said and wrapped my legs around his body, forcing him to lay flat against me.

He lifted his head and smiled so huge my heart almost imploded. "I told you I'd be home for Christmas."

"And you're a man of your word, I appreciate it."

"With you, Holly, I will always be a man of my word." It was a vow I knew I could believe. He hadn't let me down since the night of the auction.

"Get up here and kiss your wife," I demanded, need filling my tone as arousal slickened the space between my thighs.

"Gladly," he whispered against my lips, his nose brushing along my nose as his eyes sparkled with joy. "I missed you, Holly."

"Oh yeah, what did you miss?" I stretched my head the inches it took to reach his lips and kissed him briefly. "Was it my mouth?" I teased, flicking my tongue along his bottom lip. Then I arched my hips to rub against his hardening length. "Or maybe you missed something else. Hmm?" I locked my legs around him and forced his hips to press deeper along mine, creating a delicious friction.

He tunneled his hands into my hair, cupped my head and stared into my eyes as though he'd never seen anything more beautiful. "Every time I come home to you, to all we've built in just a short year, I wonder how I ever lived without you."

I ran my fingers along his hair line. "Baby, you weren't living. You were existing. I know that, because that's what I was doing too. Now we're thriving. Our careers, family, friends, and each other. We have love in all things. I don't think anyone could ever want for more."

"I love you, Holly Knight-Castellanos. Thank you for choosing me. For believing in us. Before you I was a broody asshole..."

"Before *me*? Baby let's not call a tiger a cat all of a sudden. You're still a broody asshole, you just smile and laugh more."

He chuckled and put his face to my neck, running a line of kisses up and down the column, turning the heat back up between us.

"You're right. I may still be a broody asshole, but I'm your broody asshole."

"That you are. Now please make love to your wife. I've got a whole Christmas celebration planned for us in the morning. Mom has a private brunch for us and Jonas, and then we're turning the bar into a Christmas party for all the guys. The Hounds are coming with their old ladies, the level two guys are coming...it's a whole thing and we need to get some sleep," I warned.

Bruno snorted, his hand working its way between us. The man was a master at unbuttoning jeans and getting inside them. Two fingers dove inside my heat as his thumb started working my clit just how I liked it.

"Sleep? Holly, it's time to rally, because I have two weeks of fantasies to work through with this body. You can rest when we're dead." His mouth covered mine as his fingers performed magic.

God, I missed him. "Okay, Bruno, you win."

"I always do," he smirked and took my mouth in a searing kiss before he pushed off me. "Let's start over," he said while undoing his slim tie. "Get naked, Holly."

"Rude!" I snapped, but wiggled out of my jeans, ripped my top over my head, and removed my underwear and bra. "You better be nice, or you get no dessert!"

I watched with desire as he slowly removed each item of clothing, kicking the last bit away. I stared at his gorgeous body hungrily. He did the same staring at mine.

"What's for dessert?" he asked, his voice a low rumble.

This time I smirked, laid back, and spread my legs open wide.

He fisted both of his hands and stood very still.

"I made a chocolate cake. Hungry?" I brazenly taunted.

"*Starved*," he growled and dove for the bed.

The End.

If you enjoyed *A Christmas Auction*, check out the other titles in *The Marriage Auction* universe. Start with *Madam Alana* and learn how the auction came to be, or jump right into *The Marriage Auction, Book 1*.

About Audrey Carlan

Audrey Carlan is a #1 *New York Times*, *USA Today*, and *Wall Street Journal* bestselling author. She writes stories that help the reader find themselves while falling in love. Some of her works include the worldwide phenomenon Calendar Girl serial, The Marriage Auction, and the International Guy series. Her books have been translated into over thirty-five languages across the globe. Recently her bestselling novel *Resisting Roots* was made into a PassionFlix movie.

NEWSLETTER
For new release updates and giveaway news, sign up for Audrey's newsletter: https://audreycarlan.com/sign-up

SOCIAL MEDIA
Audrey loves communicating with her readers. You can follow or contact her on any of the following:
Website: www.audreycarlan.com
Email: audrey.carlanpa@gmail.com
Facebook: https://www.facebook.com/AudreyCarlan/
Twitter: https://twitter.com/AudreyCarlan
Pinterest: https://www.pinterest.com/audreycarlan1/
Instagram: https://www.instagram.com/audreycarlan/
Tik Tok: https://www.tiktok.com/@audreycarlan
Readers Group:
https://www.facebook.com/groups/AudreyCarlanWickedHotReaders/
Book Bub: https://www.bookbub.com/authors/audrey-carlan
Goodreads:
https://www.goodreads.com/author/show/7831156.Audrey_Carlan
Amazon:
https://www.amazon.com/Audrey-Carlan/e/B00JAVVG8U/

Also From Audrey Carlan

The Marriage Auction
Book 1
Book 2
Book 3
Book 4

Madam Alana

The Marriage Auction 2
Book 1
Book 2
Book 3
Book 4

A Christmas Auction

Soul Sister Novels
Wild Child
Wild Beauty
Wild Spirit

Wish Series
What the Heart Wants
To Catch a Dream
On the Sweet Side
If Stars Were Wishes

Love Under Quarantine

Biker Beauties
Biker Babe
Biker Beloved
Biker Brit
Biker Boss

International Guy Series
Paris
New York
Copenhagen
Milan
San Francisco
Montreal
London
Berlin
Washington, D.C.
Madrid
Rio
Los Angeles

Lotus House Series
Resisting Roots
Sacred Serenity
Divine Desire
Limitless Love
Silent Sins
Intimate Intuition
Enlightened End

Trinity Trilogy
Body
Mind
Soul
Life
Fate

Calendar Girl
January
February
March
April
May
June

July
August
September
October
November
December

Falling Series
Angel Falling
London Falling

Discover More Blue Box Press authors and their amazing stories…

Go to www.TheBlueBoxPress.com for more information.

Dylan Allen
Jennifer L. Armentrout
Kristen Ashley
Xio Axelrod
Steve Berry
Lexi Blake
Audrey Carlan
Marie Force
C. W. Gortner
Heather Graham
Donna Grant
Larissa Ione
Suzanne M. Johnson
J. Kenner
Randy Susan Meyers
Jennifer Probst
Kristen Proby
Christopher Rice
M.J. Rose
Kennedy Ryan
J.R. Ward

On Behalf of Blue Box Press,

Liz Berry and Jillian Stein would like to thank ~

Steve Berry
Benjamin Stein
Kim Guidroz
Chelle Olson
Tanaka Kangara
Ann-Marie Nieves
Grace Wenk
Asha Hossain
Chris Graham
Jessica Saunders
Stacey Tardif
Suzy Baldwin
Dylan Stockton
Richard Blake
and Simon Lipskar

www.ingramcontent.com/pod-product-compliance
Lightning Source LLC
Chambersburg PA
CBHW020116310726
48970CB00002B/655